Battle Scarred Love 2

Y. Deonna

Crown Ruby Publishing

Chapter 1

Matan stared at the phone in disbelief and denial of the words his mother had just spoken. It was like he died for a second. Everything stopped and then started again. His heartbeat increased, sweat cascaded down his color-drained face, and his pulse was thumping like African drums. It was nearly impossible to breathe. The words swirled around his head like a hurricane, causing him to become dizzy with fear.

Royce was pregnant, that just couldn't be. It didn't even sound right in his head. God, please let it be a lie, he inwardly implored. He wasn't going to accept that until he saw a positive pregnancy test. Then he needed a DNA test because there was no way he impregnated what was supposed to be his future mother-in-law. He was sure women her age couldn't get pregnant. Shoot, she told him she couldn't get pregnant. He believed her old, plotting butt, but she deceived him like the serpent deceived Eve. How dumb could he be? For all he knew, this was her plan all along.

"What's wrong with you?" Fontaine asked as he walked toward him, breaking his chain of thought.

"Bruh, I just lost Royale forever," he confessed, tears falling down his light brown cheekbones. He didn't even care that the rest of his friends saw him crying. Death had to be better than what he was facing now. A child? He prayed it was Grayling's. God forgive him, but the only woman he wanted to have his babies was Royale. Life had been miserable ever since she left him.

"How?" Fontaine queried, perplexed.

"Man, my momma just called me and told me that Royce is

1

pregnant!"

"Pregnant?" all his friends chorused, their facial expressions all mirroring shock.

"What? Are you crying right now? Like, for real, you didn't wear no condom. In this day in age, you go raw?" Tataya questioned, his face balled up at his friend's stupidity. "How you let Royale's momma catch you slipping like that? Did you pull a *stealthing*? Shoot, did she?"

Matan gave him a long side-eye. No way would he ever purposely get Royce pregnant, and he sure wasn't on that *stealthing*, because tampering with condoms was dead wrong. However, he didn't wear a condom every single time they were together. "Don't even start, Tata. I don't need you cracking on me right now. This is a serious situation. I know that if my momma knows, then Royale is aware as well. Instead of my momma having some sympathy for my situation, she's planning on how to use this information to get back with Grayling."

Tataya threw his head back laughing. "Ha-ha, Ms. Rossi is messy. She is plotting and petty! Your momma on that Petty Wap! Dang, I need to start going to church. Y'all church folk worse than the sinners. Matan 'bout to be a daddy!" Tataya exclaimed, mimicking David Mann's, this is yo' granddaddy skit.

Fontaine added, "She really is on that trifling tip, but, Tata, all Christians aren't messy like that. There's a difference between Christians and church folks."

Tataya waved him off, while Matan did his best to calm his anxious nerves. He was immensely ashamed by his lustful actions. It was like his one habitual sin just completely ruined his life, but his momma was straight evil for using this to benefit herself. "Don't I know it. I'm starting to believe my momma is said church folk. She is really on a CHOT mission to get Bishop Grayling and is leaving me to rot!" he hotly expressed, before placing his head in his hands, defeated.

That allegation stunned them all into silence. Each of his friends was waiting for him to expound on what a CHOT meant, but it was Tataya who voiced it. "Expound, please," Tataya requested, his droopy, chocolate eyes widened with anticipation.

"CHOT stands for, church harlot out there," Matan stated flatly as he lifted his head and stared at each of his friends without batting an eye. His momma was all kinds of wrong to be out there acting so disgracefully and coveting after a man who didn't want her. How were her actions any different than his? At least he could blame his on being young and dumb, what was her excuse? He was going to tell his dad on her so Magnus could get in her business and put her in her place.

Tataya threw his head back and his entire body shook with amusement. His bald fade glistening under the light in the airport, and the sound of slot machines being played couldn't even drown out his deep laughter. It was drawing way too much attention, which was the last thing Matan needed. Honestly, Matan didn't see the humor in his current predicament.

"Yo, she on a CHOT mission? I can't with you, Tan. Man, you's crazy. Charles, Maurice, did you hear what this fool just called his own Ma?" he questioned as he leaned over, holding his stomach while his shoulders shook up and down. His dark skin was turning red as his guffawing intensified. Then he took a deep breath and looked back up at Matan, tears running down his crimson-stained eyeballs. "Oh, preacher boy, you just showing out now!" He shook his head but calmed himself enough to throw epic shade with a side of wisdom at Matan.

"But, check it, my dude, you're in the wrong too. As a divinity student, and Christian, didn't you ever read Joseph and the Potiphar's wife? The Potiphar's wife ran up on Joseph, she was on a CHOT mission as you termed it, but then my dude Joseph was like nah. I'm not hitting that and ran, leaving his cloak, and that's what you should have done when Royale's mom ran up on you. You shouldn't have given into the temptation. Now you got a whole world of trouble and unlike Joseph, who was unjustly cast into prison, what is happening to you is justified. You was wrong, B, and God going to do whatever He has to for you to learn from this sin you have committed."

All the guys stopped and looked at Tataya as he dropped some godly wisdom. Normally, that was Fontaine's position in the group. Matan dropped his head in shame. He should have pulled an Usain Bolt and jetted away. Royce was a formidable opponent. Still, Tataya was correct; he was in a world of trouble, but his mother wasn't making it any better. All he needed was for her to have his back and discontinue her losing battle of chasing after Grayling Chastain.

Feeling the need to lighten up the mood, Tataya came back with his signature joking. "Cheer up, Matan. I'm 'bout to trademark CHOT, and then you'll be floating in the dough and you'll be able to afford them child support payments until your baby momma's social security checks start coming. You know, 'cause she old and everything." That started the laughter up all over again, but it soon stopped again when Fontaine, wearing his trademark thick rimmed glasses went into daddy mode.

Matan started rubbing his ear because the jesting was getting to him. Thankfully, Fontaine noticed. He started shaking his head and then he lectured, "Man, just chill. Don't be disrespecting your mother like that. Tata, stop egging that on. I hate when you act ignorant in public. This isn't a joking matter. We need to help our boy." Fontaine fussed before turning his attention back to Matan. "We about to board this plane and then once you get home, you can see all this mess. Right now, the best you can do is pray and let God. I know that sounds cliché and what not, but it's the truth. You need to be on that Matthew 7:7-8 and Luke 11:9: ask, seek and knock. My brother, you need God's guidance," Fontaine offered.

"Nah, he needs that Proverbs 3:5-6, *Trust in the LORD with all your heart, and do not lean on your own understanding; in all your ways acknowledge him, and he will make straight your paths.* On a serious tip, that's why he's in trouble now. Leaning on his own understanding got him a baby on the way. We all know Royale is the smart one in the relationship. Bottom line, bruh, you should have never cheated on Royale, and until you do right by her, ain't nothing good going to come your way," Tataya countered in his Miss. Celie voice. He reenacted the movie, even putting up the two fingers at Matan, causing the others to laugh.

They were right and that hurt. He recalled Royale calling him a rock bottom vulture. He was. He felt defeated. *When Tataya calls you out for your transgressions, then you were so deep in sin, it was near impossible to get out.* He needed all of Jesus, and his situation was cliché. Had he been in God and not with another woman, he would not be part of this crap fest. Right then and there, in the airport surrounded by friends and strangers, he dropped to his knees and started to pray, and to his amazement, Fontaine placed a hand on his shoulder and fell in sync with his prayer. Matan hoped his sinfulness hadn't endangered his favor with God.

*   *

Grayling and Royale got into his Silverado HD Midnight Edition truck, both in deep contemplation as they mentally prepared themselves for the meeting with the church members. Neither knew what to expect, and both just wanted to get it done and move on.

Grayling wanted to explain to the members why he was taking some time off. He really needed to get things right, especially after she confided in him what happened to her as a child. It was remarkable how she didn't allow the negative situation to overcome her. She had a resilience that he wished he embodied. Her abuse was eating him up inside like bone cancer, and that feeling only worsened after last night. Some man touched his child and he never knew, and worse of all, Royce knew and never said a word. That would kill any man and it sure murdered a marriage.

Grayling looked back over to his daughter and inwardly smiled because her radiance was back; the opposite of what she was hours ago. Last night, Royale started off sleeping like an angel, but then something must have spooked her. Royale had a terrifying nightmare that left him holding her until she could fall back asleep again. She was literally in a fetal position on his lap, curled up like a kitten shivering and trembling for hours until she finally settled down. He mumbled her favorite verses, reminded her that God was still in charge, and made her as comfortable as he could. He didn't like how Royale's past and present were manifesting, causing her to suffer from anxiety attacks and have night terrors.

Today she was back to Royale: poised, focused and relaxed. She was indeed a remarkable young woman. Sitting on the passenger side of his truck, she gazed out the window as if seeing everything for the first time. Her long, ebony hair was braided in a halo braid. She glowed, and he wasn't sure if she was even aware of it. Grayling smiled, thankful that his daughter was home and willing to be honest with him. He was grateful that she trusted him with the truth, trusted him to protect and love her even after he had slapped her when she first flew home from Kenya. That incident seemed to be forever ago, but it scared him as much as it scared her. They had overcome that.

As a father, he really did admire Royale. Somehow, she found an inner strength to share her story with the rest of the family. He told her she didn't have to, but she said she wanted it all out because that was the only way she could truly heal and he respected that. The look of desperation, bitterness, and hurt on Patty and the General's face would haunt him to his death. He felt what they did was the lowest, most wicked of betrayals and only added another level of depravity to his wife's actions. It enraged him to the depths of his soul and he knew he had to confront Royce. In his mind, this was a pattern. He'd heard of mothers being jealous of their daughters, but he never suspected his wife had that magnitude of deceit and impiety in her being. He knew now!

All he thought about was when he told his wife he would not lose his daughter to gain her, but if he had to lose his wife, well, so be it. Right now, he didn't see how they were going to survive this storm. It was like the more he learned about Royce, the more he disliked her. He was starting to believe their entire marriage was a sham and that she only used him to get away from her overbearing and overprotective father. He was deep in his thoughts when Royale's intrepid voice sliced through his mental soliloquy.

"So, Daddy, I was thinking, after we attend the church meeting, maybe we can go see Sister Roslyn and talk to her about the lawsuit. Maybe she'd agree to the Matthew Process instead of court. I don't think she wants money; I think she's hurt by Royce's betrayal. If she can voice her concerns, express her displeasure, and feel like she's being heard, then she'll possibly let the lawsuit go. No one will ever heal if we keep carrying this burden. Someone has to let it go so the healing can begin."

Again, he was impressed by her maturity and ability to set aside her own suffering to seek to heal another. Letting out a sigh, he had to agree. Her reasoning was sound. His daughter was far wiser than he gave her credit for. "It's worth a try, sweetheart. Hopefully, we can get this over and done with quickly. The Matthew Process is a good idea."

The Matthew Process was based off the scriptures in Matthew 18:15-20 and 1 Corinthians 6:1-8. Basically, one or both parties received conflict coaching, teaching them how to resolve the dispute privately and discreetly. The process wasn't invasive but allotted both parties to air their grievances and concerns by working with each other to settle on an agreement that both would be satisfied with. He hoped that what his daughter stated would happen. Hopefully, the process would assist Roslyn in managing her emotions and any hurt she felt was inflicted by the affair Royce and Matan had because, in all honesty, she had no case. This was all Royce and Matan, and both were adults when the affair happened. If anyone ought to sue, it should be him and Royale, but neither were that narrow-minded or mean spirited.

He cleared his mind as he continued to drive to his church. His daughter had turned up the radio and Smokie Norful's "I Need You Now" began to play. It hit him right in his heart. Lord knows he needed God twenty-four seven. For him, he was drowning in ambiguity and insecurity. His wife cut him severely and he felt culpability over what his daughter faced alone. As her father, he should have known. He unconsciously hummed the tune. He didn't have the voice of his mother-in-law or his daughter, but he could hold a tune and this song spoke life to his spirit. He got lost in the song, and when he finally came to, he was pulling into the parking lot of Holy Trinity Inter-Faith Worship Center.

He could already see a lot of cars parked and he was early. He also noted that security was present, which helped him relax. It was sad, but after all the church shootings and fires, he had to implement church security measures. Most were retired police officers or ex-military.

"Are you ready, sweetheart? There is bound to be some hugs and fussing made over your appearance. They have all missed you and asked about you almost daily," Grayling told his daughter. He wanted to warn her that their church family was going to swarm her. He didn't want her to be uncomfortable.

She nodded in agreement, understanding exactly what he was saying, and he let out a relieved sigh when the prospect of being smothered with hugs and attention didn't bother her.

Just as she was getting out, Grayling noticed Roslyn's red Volvo and his heart sunk. He knew he had to have a conversation with her eventually, but he didn't want to deal with her first. Roslyn took a lot out of him and he had to be on his A game to go toe to toe with her. Right now, he just didn't have the energy it would take to deal with her.

He sedately observed her as she parked. His daughter, he noticed out of his peripheral vision, was now out of the truck and standing patiently in front of it. She had yet to notice Roslyn, and he wasn't sure how she would react to seeing Matan's mother. He turned his attention back to Roslyn. She got out of her car and called out to them. Before he could reply, his cell started to vibrate in his pocket.

He reached to retrieve it and saw that it was the facility that Royce was in, and hit ignore. He couldn't deal with her now either, but as soon as he did, it started ringing again. That had him mystified and all kinds of crazy thoughts encumbered his mind.

"Grayling!" Roslyn hollered as if he didn't hear her call his name the first time. He put up one finger, signaling for her to wait while he answered his cell phone.

"Hello?"

"Bishop Chastain, hello, thank God you answered." The voice went from high-pitch stressed to a relieved, calming tone.

"Who is this?" He knew it wasn't his wife.

"Oh, sorry. This is Janice, your wife's counselor. Something happened today and your wife was assaulted by a visitor and we had to take her to the hospital. Can you come? She is asking for you."

Before he could reply, Roslyn was on his face, and by the way, she looked like something was really bothering her, but she would have to wait her turn. He was still trying to understand why Janice was calling him.

"Grayling, please, I need to speak to you. It's extremely important."

"Hold on, Rossi." He mentally chided himself as he noticed how she beamed when he acknowledged her by the pet name, he used to call her back in the day. He prayed she didn't read too much into it. Honestly, there was nothing between them except the air. "What were you saying, Janice?" As she repeated herself, he noticed how Roslyn frowned.

"It seems like she's okay. I have to attend some church business and I'll get there when I can."

"It's imperative that you get here now," Janice persisted.

He could hear the impatience in her tone, but he wasn't going to give in. Royce would have to wait. "Why? Didn't you just say she was fine, and that they took her as a precaution?" It couldn't have been that serious because Janice never stated that the police were called or that his wife was hurt.

"She's asking for you."

Grayling closed his eyes and let out an exasperated sigh. That woman always found a way to make herself matter more than anyone else. Royce really was not a priority now. Her mouth was reckless and her actions were juvenile. Whatever caused her to be hospitalized was more than likely due to her inability to hush. "I'll get there when I can, but if you need someone there now, just call her parents. I have to go now, Janice." He hung up. Taking a deep breath, he turned his attention back to Roslyn and asked,

"What did you need to tell me?" She was flushed, her toffee-colored skin reddened and he saw what looked like bruising around her neck and forearm, which he hadn't noticed before. Just as he was about to question her as to what happened, she cut him off and began to speak.

"I went to see Royce today to ask her to refrain from calling my son. She has contacted him and he asked her not to do so. Anyway, when I was there, she and I had words and things got a little out of hand. Actually, we had a physical altercation, I'm ashamed to admit. However, Janice informed me that Royce is pregnant."

"What?" Royale queried. Her body instantly encumbered by the words spoken. Her honey copper eyes were floating in unshed tears at the unexpected news.

His daughter had been so quiet that he momentarily forgot she was present. Just like him, she didn't take the news well. Grayling stumbled back, hitting his truck. Had he heard correctly? His wife was pregnant, which meant she had to know before she started her treatment, so why didn't she tell him. He felt himself become overheated as the words penetrated his mind. That hurt, that brutally hurt and he felt his heart detaching from the rest of his body.

"So...so is Matan the father?" he asked for clarity. This couldn't be happening. It was like every day he woke, the situation expanded and got worse by the minute. He was barely making it and seeing his daughter cry disturbed him more. He sucked up his pain as best he could to be strong for his daughter.

Looking hopeless and feeling helpless, Roslyn took a deep breath before replying. "Grayling, I don't know. I can only assume. I'm just as upset and flabbergasted as you. I know Royce hates me, but what has Matan and Royale ever done for her to be so calculating and insidious? Lord have mercy. When will this be over?" she wept.

He honestly had no answer for her, but for the first time, he saw sincere emotions coming from Roslyn. This was taking a toll on her as well. He wondered had she spoken to Magnus, Matan's biological father, about the issue. Even though she swore he was no good, he loved his son and cared about Roslyn as well, but she was so hung up on the past she couldn't see the truth.

"That's disgusting. With all we have going on, she's adding a child to the mix. Oh, God, we need you now," Royale bemoaned, and Grayling reached out and pulled her into a side embrace and Roslyn fell into his chest. He wanted this nightmare to end, but it kept getting more calamitous and he was sure that the child his wife was carrying wasn't his and that, believe it or not, broke his heart. As much as he loathed all the horrible actions, she had committed against him, their marriage and family, he still loved his wife. He was a fool, or so he felt like one.

"I'm so sorry, Grayling. I didn't raise him that way. I never wanted to sue, I just—"

"I know, Rossi. Now that I can see through my own indignation, I understand that you were just dispirited and felt betrayed. I forgive you for that. Just calm down and we can work through it later. However, right now, I need a favor. Go in and let only the church members know that Royce is in the hospital and that I'm going to check on her and they can reschedule for about seven o'clock tonight." He didn't want to postpone it any longer. It needed to happen soon so he could handle the escalating problems he had at home.

"Of course, Gray, I'll be discreet. You can count on me. I just want to aid you in any way that I can," Roslyn promised.

Grayling nodded to her and she turned to leave, then he turned toward his daughter. "I'm sorry, baby." She collapsed her head onto his chest and he worried about her having an anxiety attack. "Royale, take some deep breaths. I don't want this to trigger an anxiety attack. As long as we place God first, we can get through any obstacle in our way," he told her.

After finding out about her suffering from anxiety attacks, he looked up the condition to see what it was about. Apparently, when a person was having an attack, their heart raced, skin became flushed, and they had chest pains and difficulty breathing. He wanted to prevent that from happening. He didn't want her to allow these setbacks to harm her mentally.

"I'm okay, Daddy. Let's just go and see what this is all about."

He escorted her to the passenger side of his truck and assisted her into the truck before getting into the driver's side. Once they were settled, he drove to the hospital to see what mess Royce was into now. Grayling was sure after this conversation; he would be seeking out a divorce attorney. That was the last thing he wanted to do, but how could their marriage survive this? Infidelity was one thing, but a baby and one she tried to hide? She had ample opportunity to tell him about her pregnancy and chose not to do so. How could she reach out to Matan to inform him before having a conversation with her own husband? Probably because the child belonged to Matan.

Chapter 2

Khan finally finished up at the police station. He did inform them that he had video footage and gave them a copy, but he kept the original. He knew that some of the police officers on the force were still loyal to his dad and shared his father's beliefs, so he wasn't sure who he could trust. However, he knew the truth. He knew that his father wanted him to become full of hate and preach white power, but that wasn't and never would be him. Now, he was attempting to bully and threaten him, but Khan wasn't bothered. He had someone worth fighting for and he would protect Royale at all cost.

There was a lot on Khan's mind, and he was thankful that Nehemiah and Canton were already present at his business, overseeing the progress. So, before Khan headed back to them to get a visual on the progress, he went to visit his mother. He hadn't been to her grave in a few days, but Mama Byse kept it clean all the time. He was thankful for her dedication to him and his mother in life and in death.

Once he arrived at his mother's headstone, he sat Indian style and rested reticently while he collected his thoughts. After five minutes, he began speaking as if his mother was sitting down in front of him. It had been years since he actually talked to her. Mostly out of guilt, because he still blamed himself for allowing her to die. He missed her. He missed her scent, her dulcet voice and the way she hummed him Welsh lullabies. He missed the warmth of her skin and the humming of her heart when she held him and read him books. He inhaled one deep breath and exhaled one tear. That was all he allowed to escape before sharing with her all the ways his life had altered.

He told her about Kalid contacting him and requesting that he come for a visit so he could find out the truth and not the alternative facts he'd been fed as a child. Then, he told her about his father, and his vendetta against an entire race of people because of the actions of one. Finally, he ended with Royale, who had become his happiness and joy. Just saying her name made the acrimony in him diminish. He loved her and that was crazy. Who fell in love with someone they'd known less than a week? Him. He really didn't care what anyone else thought. For far too long, he had been raised in hate and hostility, and he needed love like California needed rain in the dry season. He needed Royale and God willing, he would have her.

"I love her, mom. I know it's crazy. It hasn't even been two weeks, but like you said, when you know, you know. Royale is God's gift to me and I will treasure her until my dying day. She's a rare gem and I'm so thankful to have her in my life.

"She was hurt by her ex and her mother. They had an affair and I think it left her a little jaded, but when we're together, our problems don't exist. Just us. I trust her, and she trusts me. I just need to get Pops out of my life. I won't let him take her from me, mom. I won't lose her like I lost you. I'll fight for her like I should have fought for you. That's my vow," he confessed.

He closed his eyes as the wind kissed his back. He was deep in the moment, thinking about how much his mother would have loved Royale. As if he mentally summoned Royale, his cell started to ring and he quickly answered when her face popped up.

"Hey, Honey Drop." He did his best to lift the emotion out of his voice. He didn't want to worry her. She had this gift, this sixth sense of knowing when something was bothering him.

"Khan." Her voice was hoarse and full of distress. That immediately alarmed him. His first mind told him it had to do with Matan and her mother. If Matan was giving her a hard time, then he would see that other side of Khan; it wasn't pretty. He didn't inherit his father's hate, but he had his temper and he meant what he said. Royale was dealing with a man and anyone who came for her, came for him. He would protect the one he loved.

"What's wrong, Royale?"

"Oh, my goodness, Khan. There's so much, but I can't get into it all right now. Basically, my dad and I, we made up and we were going to church for a meeting when Matan's mother, Sister Roslyn, came up to us. She told us that she and Royce got into a rumble and that Royce is pregnant and she thinks it's Matan's. Can you believe that? As if things aren't chaotic enough, now there is a child involved."

He had to pull the cell phone from his ear and look at it as if Royale could see him. That wasn't where he expected the conversation to go. He really thought she was going to tell him something else, but that, he didn't see coming. "I'm sorry, honey. I can't imagine how devastating that information must have been. I can come to you. I want to come and be there for you," Khan offered.

"No, you have enough on your plate. I just needed to talk to someone. I hope I didn't interrupt anything."

He gave a humorless chuckle. She was always so thoughtful, but he was worried about her. "You didn't. Let me come see you, then you can ride back with me Friday night and I'll go talk to Kalid, and after that, we can just chill. I miss you."

"I miss you too. I'll send you my address and you can let me know when you're coming. Thank you, Khan."

"Anytime. I'll see you soon. Call me if you need me. The guys and I are just cleaning up, but my teams are working, so my old man didn't hurt my business. If anything, he helped my business get free advertisement."

"I like the way you view setbacks, but be careful, Khan. I feel like if he'll burn your business and threaten the Byses with nooses, then he will become more aggressive. I'm a peaceful woman, but if he comes for you again, I'll have to show out. Let me inform you, ain't nothing worse than a woman with her Bible and a prayer. He doesn't want it!"

He chortled. He loved hearing her getting all riled up over his safety. "That won't be necessary, but it's good to know you have my back."

"Always, and don't you forget it. Look, I should go now. My dad is waving at me to come with him. We have a meeting tonight at church, but I'll try to call before then."

"Okay, bye, Honey Drop." They hung up and then Khan blew a kiss to his mother and dropped his head in prayer before leaving.

* *

Royale hopped out of her father's truck and strolled toward him. The pair walked hand in hand into the hospital. It reminded her of when she was a child and they would walk into church together. Back then, when he was home, she'd follow him around like a puppy. He always felt safe to her, and that's exactly what she needed to feel now. Parts of her wanted to forgive her mother, while another part wanted to rip her a new one.

It hurt.

She was deeply scarred, probably beyond repair by her mother's actions with Larry, Matan and how she forced Royale to lie to her father by omission. It was time to clean the dirty laundry and bring it all to the forefront. Either they would survive or perish, she didn't know which, but she knew praying was always the answer.

It was her father's commanding voice that pulled her from her invasive thoughts. He asked the information clerk what room Royce was in. Once they had that information, they went to the elevator and pressed the three to go to the third floor. For some reason, Royale's heart was pounding, causing her to breathe unevenly. This was not the time to have an anxiety attack.

Instantly, her father turned to her with concerned eyes. She felt so embarrassed to allow this situation to cause her to be anxious. Her father placed both hands on either side of her head and talked comfortably to her, telling her to breathe slowly and just focus on his voice. It was okay, and no matter what happened, they would get through it. She nodded in understanding as the doors slid open. She was thankful that it was only her and her father on the elevator.

"Royale, if you can't handle this, it's okay to sit in the waiting room. You don't have to see Royce until you're ready. You have my word that I won't allow her or anyone else to harm you, psychologically or physically. That's my vow to you."

"Okay." She knew that he meant the words he spoke because that little vein in his forehead was protruding.

"Are you ready?"

"Yes, sir."

Royale took two more deep breaths and started praying as she and her father strolled down the hall, bypassing the nurses' station and arrived at her mother's room. It was like walking the Green Mile. She hadn't seen her vessel in nine weeks. Now she was about to see her and the woman was carrying her ex-boyfriend's child. Could it get any worse than this? Then she smacked herself in the head. *Never ask a question you don't want the answer to*, she mentally chided herself.

"Honey, you're about to break my hand in two," Grayling told his daughter calmly, although his face was betraying him as it was balled up in pain.

She quickly let go and apologized. They continued roaming until they arrived at Royce's room. When they entered through the door, Royale couldn't believe her eyes. The way Janice went on, she expected some beeping machinery, but that's not what she found. Instead, it was like a cast reunion for the *First Ladies of DC*, all they were missing was a reunion host. All of them were in there and Royce was eating up the attention, but what angered Royale the most was seeing Marc. She recalled how he bullied Rina. He was going to pay for that. She didn't even play a little bit with Rina and Marc needed to apologize for his aggressive tactics.

Royale crossed her arms and narrowed her honey copper eyes as she surveyed the women and Marc. It took a moment, but the loud chatter stopped once Uma noticed Royale and her father at the door. Uma's long, oval face dropped, and that started a domino effect that stopped with Royce, who was eating up the attention until she saw Royale and Grayling. Then she had the nerve to look distressed and put on that fake hurt face. The kind of face a Pug dog has that looks so cute on them. Well, Royce had it down pat, but it wasn't working for her.

In that moment, Royale heard and saw only Royce. All that putting the past behind them and moving forward, forgotten. This had been a long time coming, the first showdown between mother and daughter. Royale wasn't one to give into anger, but she was volcanic hot when she saw Royce. Just like that, she was sucked back into time, back when she caught Matan and Royce laid up in a precarious position. She did her best to shake it off. She swallowed hard, keeping the bile from rising in her throat. Her father reached out and gently placed his warm hand on hers as if he sensed the rumbling in her heart. It was his touch that re-laxed the beating percussion that she called a heartbeat.

"Oh, my goodness, Royale. You look stunning, sweetheart. Heartbreak didn't break you with your pretty self. When did you get back in town?" Coletta asked, another of Royce's cast mates. She was as fake as they came. She rocked her twenty-four-inch Brazilian weave and had on way too much makeup, which made her face look oily. As always, she was wearing some expensive designer clothing and Red Bottom heels.

Royale offered her a forced smile but remained silent, her eyes glaring at Royce. It was clear that she was fine and was milking this for all it was worth. If she could entertain these people and smile up in their faces, then she didn't need to be in the hos-pital. There were signs of an altercation, but nothing seemed bad enough for her to be admitted to the hospital. It looked like Sis-ter Roslyn got a good grip on her because she had some whelps and bruises around her neck. It kind of saddened her that adult women of God were acting like unsaved, immature little girls.

"Ladies, and Marc, if you could all leave us, I would appre-ciate it," Grayling requested. Royale noticed how he put on his signature bishop-ness upon the request. The women got up, all obviously swooning over her father. She didn't know if it was his dark skin, his deep voice, or Morris Chestnut looks, but bishops had groupies just like dope boys, actors, and musicians. It seemed people were attracted to power, and it didn't help that her father was handsome.

"Anything for you, Grayling. We've missed you," Coletta cooed, looking Grayling up and down, making Royale feel uncomfortable for him. Then, as if she wasn't bold enough, she strutted up to Grayling like a peacock and placed her hand wantonly on his left bicep. "Oh, you've been working out," she noted as she squeezed his arm. Coletta's eyes were full of lust and longing. She bit the bottom of her lip and leaned her head as if she were preparing to kiss Grayling. "We haven't seen or heard from you in a while, and I just wanted to personally tell you that if you need anything, and I mean anything, just give me a call," she told him in a hypnotic, sultry, singsong voice of Shug in *The Color Purple*. Then she looked over at Royale as if she were an afterthought before replying, "You too, sweetie."

"Coletta!" Royce's alto voice came out cold and harsh. Her eyes darkened in warning to her co-star. "Leave, I'm sure your husband and children miss you."

Just as Royce called her out, Coletta smirked and winked at Grayling before sashaying out the door. She was throwing her hips so hard, Royale thought they would pop out of place. Royale just shook her head at the woman being so unabashed and extra. She was a married woman and acting thirsty like she didn't have a man at home. Royale wanted to drop Psalm 42:2 on her and tell her that her soul needed to be thirsting for God, and not her father, but she kept that to herself. Thankfully, the rest of the women left with less fanfare, and only Marc remained. He was really trying it. Like, really, who feared Marc? He was simply a leech and he and Royce were two rotten peas in a pod.

"My daddy meant you also, Marc, but make sure you remain available. You and I need to have a personal conversation soon," Royale deadpanned, her eyes dripping with frigidness and hardened like ice while glaring at him. Nobody was messing her sister over after what Strom did to her.

"Royale, sweetie, you sound a little hostile with a side of bitter. I hope I haven't upset you. We're friends," he replied, fluttering his eyelashes.

"Marc, don't attempt to throw shade or check my child. It won't end well for you. You're the one with guttersnipe tendencies. Now, leave, and don't make me ask a third time. I'm not here on Bishop business, and you can take that however you like," Grayling retorted, his indifferent demeanor hardened and his eyes turned stoned.

Royale almost laughed at how quickly Marc collected his belongings. He leaned over and whispered something in Royce's ear before excusing himself and exiting out of the room. He didn't want to witness the street come out of her daddy. He'd better pray that Antwon didn't roll up on him because he didn't mind getting a little dirty if necessary.

It was still for a moment, neither knowing how to start the conversation that needed to be had. Royale watched both her parents, but her concern was only for her father. Her heart wouldn't allow her to feel remorse, pity or empathy for her vessel. Royale mimicked her father's battle stance as well as his unreadable facial expression. It was Royce who broke the silence.

"Gray, I'm glad you came. I was so scared," she started, her dark eyes looking humbling at Grayling's, causing Royale to roll her eyes.

Royce was always a performer. It sure was comical how she was suddenly afraid now that they were present. She seemed right as rain when her castmates were present.

Before his mouth could open, Royale could feel the change come over him. He was probably madder than she was. He was dealing with the past and the present all at once. Royce had ripped her father's heart out and nobody knew why she sought outside affairs or why she allowed Larry to do what he did to Royale. All of that had to be meandering in his mind, making her wish she could carry his pain.

Royale observed silently as her father closed the hospital door before turning back around. His face was ice cold; it was like he went through a transformation that quickly. He pulled out a chair and directed Royale to sit down, which she did. There was a torrent of emotions flowing through Royale. It was most likely best that she be seated and not standing up just in case the situation became intense. She feared she would charge Royce and finish off what Roslyn started. That wasn't the godly way to handle the issues, nor was it respectful. To compose her anxious nerves, she started rubbing her thighs in a scratching motion.

Royale was baffled by the pregnancy announcement, but also, she was perturbed that her vessel pretended to want her marriage to work, all the while she was still reaching out to Matan. Royale had no idea what her endgame was, but she was going to lose on both counts if she didn't get it together.

Grayling stood in front of Royale, as if protecting her from Royce's gaze. Then he crossed his muscled arms before finally speaking, "Scared?"

It sounded like a question, statement, and accusation all at once. That prompted Royale to lean around her father to see Royce's reaction. Royce seemed nervous, skittish, and puzzled by Grayling's response. So, Royale just leaned back and watched whatever was about to unfold without any interference. She and Royce would have their moment, but for now, her father needed to relieve the tension, pain, and betrayal off his chest, and she was going to let him do just that.

"Yes, scared," she confirmed before continuing. "Roslyn assaulted me. I ought to press criminal charges. Can you believe she attacked me? She's supposed to be a woman of God. She's just one of them church folk, she's not really saved, acting like a savage."

"Mmhm. So, you feared Roslyn, kind of like my daughter feared Larry. Instead of acting like a Proverbs 31 woman and being saintly, you chose to act like a thirsty, salty savage. No, I take that back, you weren't thirsty, you were desiccated and I guess all those men were your Gatorade. You needed to replenish your electrolytes, right?" he clapped back, causing the hair on the back of Royale's neck to rise and her eyes to widen in surprise. One part of her wanted to laugh at her father's epic shade, but the other part of her was just too flabbergasted to move.

Here is why she was astounded. Reason one, she didn't know her daddy knew how to correctly use slang terminology like *savage, salty* and *thirsty*, plus she was still shocked that he called Marc a guttersnipe. With all her education, she had never even heard that word before. It just blew her mind that the Bishop was with the times. Reason two, she didn't know he was going to confront her about the Larry situation. Reason three, he told Royce she was desiccated, like completely dried out and said she needed to replenish her electrolytes, now it was her dad who had gone savage. He was killing Royce softly. Then again, he did inform Marc he wasn't here on Bishop business. Bishop came to slay, not to pray. Oh, it was about to go down. Her daddy was about to pounce and all she could do was sit by quietly and sip all the tea.

Royale watched her father's body language shift. He was annoyed by Royce's act of innocence and claim of being a victim. It looked like her dad was going for the jugular. So, she rearranged herself in the chair, arms crossed in solidarity while saying a silent prayer. She had never seen this side of her father and she was a little nervous.

Royce's reaction was priceless. She turned every shade of red known to man, and her eyes looked like they were bugged out, which made her look even more like a Pug puppy. Just as quickly as she tried to pull her face together, Royale leaned around her father and glared, wondering how Royce was going to lie her way out of this one.

"Grayling, I...I...I don't know what she told you, but honey, she was a child. She's remembering it all wrong," she refuted, her face finally overcoming the shock of the allegation Grayling charged her with. Royale was unimpressed. Was that the best she had? Was she going to turn this into 'he said, she said'? She wasn't a child anymore, and she was more than willing to stand up to her mother, especially since her father knew the truth and had her back.

"Really, because she seemed to recall it quite vividly with remarkable accuracy. It seems you're the one who has trouble recapturing the memories, and you're the only one to gain anything by having selective amnesia. You told me that it was ten years when it was more like sixteen years unless you were taking breaks in between your affairs. I really don't care at this point. However, you'll not call my child a liar," he growled.

"How dare you speak so condescendingly to me? I'm your wife, Gray. It was us before it was ever anyone else." He didn't even reply to her question. Instead, he acted like she hadn't even asked it, but then again, he might not have heard her over the lies she was telling.

Royale smiled at her father champing her. Had they been in church, this would have been an *Amen* moment followed by *say it's so, Bishop*, while waving the church fan, but this wasn't the time or place, so she chilled. When it all first happened, she felt like her father was on Royce's side, but now that the truth was slowly unfolding, he was seeing her for the fraud she was.

"Royale, honey, tell your father the truth," Royce demanded, putting her Miss America face back on and calming her anxiety. Royale had to give it to Royce, that woman played her character to the end. She missed her calling as an actress because that was all she was doing, acting.

Royale mentally snapped at her mother's request. "Royce, honey, I did tell the truth. You should try it sometimes," Royale quipped saucily as she stood up. There was something about Royce, the woman who birthed her, attempting to call her a liar that just unleashed the floodgates. That old feeling of indignity, betrayal, and affliction overcame her.

She was momentarily back in that dark orb where Leering Larry was touching her, whispering unwanted words in her ear, and that woman who was supposed to be her mother allowed it. She was livid at the accusation that *she* was the one lying. However, as much as she didn't want to go hard on her, a part of her wanted to serve Royce the same pungent meal she had served others. Before she knew it, she was right at Royce's bedside. Only

God knows how she got there because she honestly didn't recall moving.

Royale could see the uncertainty in Royce's eyes and felt the coldness that lingered in her own eyes. Was that fear Royce was showing? Royale shook her head in dismay and before she could think, her mouth got a severe case of vocal diarrhea.

"You're pathetic. I can't believe I kept all your dirty little secrets just because I wanted your approval, love, and respect. I no longer care. You can't manipulate me, you can't hurt me, and you no longer exist to me. That's as nice as I can be without being like you. I hope you treat the baby you're pregnant with now better than you treated me. That ought to be interesting, you and Matan raising a baby together." Then she paused and shook her head as she had a flash of what that family unit would look like before continuing.

"At your age, I know there are risks, and I don't want to stress the fetus. I won't be seeing you again because you still aren't sorry for the shame and pain you've caused. But I pray that God gives you everything you have given your family over the years. I hear God's vengeance is far better than anything a man can think of. Bye, Royce," Royale sneered more callously than she thought she was capable of. It felt good to finally say what was on her heart and not sit timidly by and allow her mother to disrespect her.

Then she turned to her father. "Daddy, I'll be in the truck, take as long as you need. I have enough to entertain myself for hours," she told him and leaned to kiss his cheek.

"I won't be long, sweetheart," he replied and kissed her forehead.

* *

Grayling watched his daughter saunter out, his heart going out to her. He knew it was the pain speaking, but there was truth in her words. He only hoped that some of what Royale said penetrated Royce's walls.

Taking a deep breath, he turned his gaze toward Royce, who looked like her entire world was crumbling, but what did she expect when the truth came out? Shaking his head, he stayed silent and glanced at his wife. His dark eyes narrowed as he attempted to understand how they had gotten to this place in their marriage. He just couldn't find the words to illustrate his feelings, but that didn't matter because it was Royce who interrupted the quietude.

"Grayling, I'm sorry."

He almost chuckled at her weak and ineffective apology. He cracked his neck and fingers to relieve some of the mounting pressure that had overtaken him at her lie. He didn't acknowledge her apology because he didn't believe she was sorry. "Who is the father?"

He saw the crestfallen look on her face and prepared for her to tell him what he suspected, which was the child belonged to Matan.

"I honestly don't know. I only reached out to Matan to let him know. I knew that you weren't speaking to me, but I was planning on telling you as well. I feel like it's yours. I know you always wanted another child."

He started shaking his head before she completed her last sentence. He could literally smell the manipulation; it smelt like fire and brimstone. "Don't, Royce. Don't do that. You know, when the affair with Matan came to light, I was upset and hurt, but I was willing. I was willing to do what I had to do to get my family back, forgive you and stand as a united front. Then you confessed to these other emotional affairs, and that cracked my heart, but my love for you kept my heart from fully breaking. I prayed to God to mend me. I thought maybe I'd done wrong and for that, I needed to seek forgiveness and shoulder some of the responsibility. However, as always, you went too far, and the truth came out about you reaching out to Strom, knowing the kind of man he is, and to add salt to the gaping wound, you suggested I was having a sexual relationship with my sister." He paused on that one because it still broke his heart that she would even speak that lie. Taking a deep breath, he continued.

"That added more cracks to my heart, but there were still

pieces there because I know how you react when cornered. I know you hit way below the belt, so I was willing, and then my baby..." His voice cracked and tears followed. "My daughter tells me she was fondled and touched in an inappropriate manner that led to her almost being raped and you blamed her. That ripped my heart out and made my soul bleed. Now you're suggesting this child you're carrying might be mine or Matan's because you slept with us both, apparently not using protection. Wow! Good for you, my STD panel came back all negatives because if you had given me something, we wouldn't be conversing now."

"Gray."

"Hush, Royce!" He slashed his hand through the air, irritated by her unsolicited interruption. "You don't speak, and you don't call me Gray. I don't want to hear your voice. All you need to do from this moment on is listen and listen well because I won't be repeating myself. I'm done. I don't care what people say or think. We're not staying married because you don't understand what marriage is. Everything isn't about you, but you sure make it that way. I loved you, Ro. I loved you more than myself and this is what we've come to now." He let out a priggish cackle before continuing, his hands coming together like a temple resting on his lips as he contemplated his final words. "I don't know what game or games you're playing, but you just played your last hand with me, and you lose.

"When they release you, I suggest you go back to the rehab facility and complete your program. Not for your family or me, but for yourself, because you need help. Maybe you should extend your stay, but at any rate, whenever you're released, you aren't welcome back to my home. You can stay with your parents, Marc, or even Matan. I don't care, but you can't come back to the home we used to share. Your belongings will be shipped to your parents' house. My attorney will be in contact about the divorce, and if that is my child, then I will fight you for full custody. You've already nearly ruined Royale, I won't allow you to hurt this child as well. Goodbye, Royce," he lectured and then turned around and stormed out, not even giving her a second glance. They were over.

As he exited, the tears continued to flow. She did what no woman ever had; she broke his heart. He thought they had the kind of love that would overcome anything. Theirs was a battle scarred love, but he didn't do secrets and lies because they were the death of a marriage. God forgive him, but he didn't want a woman who didn't want him. He refused to fight a losing battle.

Chapter 3

Matan landed in Virginia and the entire flight from Las Vegas to home had his mind all kinds of crazy. He floated between animosity, confusion, and distress. His mother really cared more about getting Grayling than about her own son.

He was aggravated. It could very well be Grayling's baby because he was sure she was still having a sexual relationship with her husband. At least he hoped so.

He couldn't shake the madness. Then he was contemplating worse case scenarios and wondered if Grayling would kill him or have Antwon kill him if the baby Royce was carrying belonged to him.

No parts of him wanted to be a father, and every part of him wanted Royale, but if she found out about this, there would be no coming back. That was something he couldn't accept.

He grabbed the sides of his head to hush the voices in his mind. Once he was calm, he turned to his best friend with his mind made up. It was time to face his worst mistake. "Fontaine, come with me to the hospital. Ma texted me where Royce is and I need to see about this baby."

"Bruh, you sure 'bout that? I mean, maybe we oughta head home first before you go see that woman. For all you know, Royale and Bishop Chastain might be there, and then what?"

"Taine, if you don't take me, then I'll take myself, but I'ma see Royce today."

Fontaine nodded. "Fine, I ain't letting you go up in there alone.

You do stupid stuff when I leave you unsupervised. Tan, I hope we don't live to regret this, let's go."

*   *

Royce sat in her hospital bed in a state of shock, not believing what had just transpired. When had Royale become so fierce? She knew her good girl act was just that, an act. After being properly scolded by her husband, or soon to be ex-husband from the way they left things, had her all in her feelings. He didn't even let her defend herself, he just said goodbye. She still couldn't believe that Royale told her father about Larry and all the other men. She thought for sure Royale would never tell, she made sure of it. Larry didn't succeed in raping her, he only touched her and now Royale was using that situation to break up their family. Sure, she didn't help the situation when she alleged that Gwendolyn and Grayling had an affair, but she was cornered, and when she felt cornered, she lashed out. He knew that. So, it shouldn't be a factor in his dismissing her. She knew it was a lie when it left her lips, but she wanted to hurt him, but now she was the one hurting.

How had it all gone so wrong? If Royale had kept her mouth shut, she could have had Grayling wrapped back around her finger, but no, Royale wanted to be petty. That was okay, she would find a way to get what she wanted. She wasn't losing her husband and she darn sure wasn't going to allow Roslyn to slide into her role as wife, mother, and first lady. Nor was she going to permit her daughter to take Grayling from her either. Her mind quickly started to plot what her next moves needed to be.

"Royce!" her mother's country-accented voice interjected her thoughts. That professional vernacular she utilized when she was at award shows, interviews, and speaking engagements, gone. This was about to be dramatic. Everything in Royce's being was hoping it was a dream and that her mother wasn't in her room, but as she languidly swung her head, there was her mother and father. Today was officially the worse day of her life.

Their eyes said it all. They knew, or so they thought they knew. It wasn't like she was born bitter and narcissistic; it was a defense mechanism she developed to save herself. Lord knows there were monsters in this world and they didn't look like the boogieman, they looked like Bible-toting, Jesus loving followers. Burying the darkness, she swore to never allow to rise, she glared at her mother. "Yes, mother?" she queried dumbly.

"What have you done?"

"Nothing, I was attacked by my husband's ex-girlfriend and only attempted to defend myself. Was I supposed to allow her unlimited access to my body and allow her to beat me? Why, because she never got over her broken heart? I'll not apologize for protecting myself, it isn't like anyone else is."

"That woman was his high school girlfriend, stop acting like that man is still in love with her or vice versa. You tried it, but I'm not falling for it. You brought all this on yourself. This pregnancy, your daughter running away, and the ire of your husband. How could you allow your own daughter to be sexually accosted, blame her and then threaten her to keep it all a secret? Do you know the mental issues that causes? My God, who are you really, Royce? I've prayed for you and will continue to do so. However, at every turn, the evil madness that is you gets harder and harder to forgive. No one can help you if you continue to keep secrets, tell lies and refuse to be held accountable. That's not how Christians operate. You are acting like unsaved church folks; get your life before you lose everything," Patty fussed angrily.

Royce's eyes went dark and icy. Her mother's voice sounded like nails on a chalkboard. It was irritating to her entire being. She could take no more of being berated and disrespected. First, Royale, then Gray, and now her mother? That was it, she was pissed. "Okay, mother, here's the truth," she growled sarcastically, her eyes squinting and her small hands balled in anger. She could feel the heat overtake her body and she prepared to give them the information they so desperately wanted. "I'm a screw up because of Lance Kirkland, remember him? Daddy's best friend and personal lawyer until he became a district court judge. Did you know that Lance had a thing for young black girls who wore ponytails? What happened to Royale wasn't anything compared to what happened to me.

"From the age of twelve to almost seventeen, I was Lance's morning, noon and night delight. He got me pregnant and forced me to have an abortion, and where was my mother? She was making records and singing gospel songs to sold out crowds. Where was my father? He was busy building the foundation for his political career. I was just in between. My good old godfather used your detractions to his sick benefit. He was infatuated with me.

"So, sorry I didn't react the way you think I should have when I found out about Larry. Anyway, the only reason I didn't notify the police about Larry was because I didn't think our family could survive the scandal. Besides, he didn't rape her and she didn't get pregnant nor was she forced to have an abortion at sixteen. All he did was fondle her, and when he tried to rape her, I stopped it. I did let him have it because I can't stand people who hurt children, and yes, I hollered at her too. I told her to never let anyone touch her. She's smart, darn near genius status, she should have told me when it first happened.

"Honestly, I did more for Royale than my parents did for me," she spat. Goodness, her parents were irking her soul, but she wasn't done yet. She was sitting straight up on the edge of the bed, eyeing both her parents. Their lack of action was part of her actions, so they had to blame themselves as well.

She licked her lips and continued her tirade. "How about instead of judging me, you take a moment and look in the mirror, mother. I am what I was created to be. I was scarred to my soul, terrified and broken. Who was there for me? Nobody, not one living soul until I met Grayling. Don't attack my character when you failed to keep me safe. Now, if you don't like how I've been behaving, then leave. I'm sick of people coming in here, speaking to me so disrespectfully and treating me like a pile of dung. I suffered in silence for nearly five years and had a baby taken from me. I was forced to kill my own child. I got over it, Royale will too, and if not, well, she's not as strong as I thought she was." What was the saying, sometimes people have a fire in their hearts and speak sparks? Well, she spoke volcanic lava. They could all get it. She was done being the punching bag.

Silence.

You could hear a spider crawling on cotton. Honestly, Royce would have taken that to her grave. Only two people knew about the sexual abuse, but never that she got pregnant or had an abortion. She never wanted anyone to know that she was forced to have an abortion and she didn't want them to know that she had sex with Lance, a man old enough to be her father. After so many years, she started to like it. Not the sex, but the attention. Since there was no one to express her feelings to, she did what felt good. Back in the day, Lance felt good.

Royce liked that she mattered to Lance, but when she told him she was having his child, she wasn't prepared for his reaction. He was angry and called her every kind of nasty name before declaring the child wasn't his. It wounded her. Now it felt like a replay after she and Grayling had it out. He was doubtful that the child she carried now was his. It made her feel like that scared sixteen-year-old all over again, but worse than that, he let her know he didn't want her anymore. Her greatest fear was being unwanted.

Grayling didn't even know that he was penetrating her armor and now her mother finished ripping it off. For so long, she chased that feeling of worth and attention. Sex was what she had to offer and her way of feeling worthy. Grayling was the first and only man who saw beyond her body. He wanted her mind, body, and soul and now her immature actions put their marriage in jeopardy. The idea of being alone terrified her. Grayling had given her what she needed up and until his calling for the Lord was stronger than his love for her. So, she sought it out in other men. It was never supposed to go on so long, and she really hadn't meant to seek Matan, but he was young, virile, attentive and so easy to manipulate. It was a game, a game that had gotten out of control.

"Royce, Lance Kirkland is dead. Are you accusing him of being a pedophile, and if so, why have you waited so long to share this information? Is this another manipulation tactic?" her father questioned in an accusatory tone.

"No. It's the truth. I knew it was wrong, but he loved me, or so I thought. I believed the lies he told me, memorized them as if they were commandments, and when I got pregnant, the real beast that was him was revealed. I knew his body as intimately as I knew my own. If you want proof, ask his daughter, Mahogany Kirkland-Fields. She reached out after all this mess and asked me how I was. She's a victim advocate for sexual assault survivors. It's a way to absolve the guilt of knowing what her father was doing to me."

"No. Father God, no." Patty exhaled as she collapsed in the chair that once held Royale. She clutched her black cultured Tahitian pearl necklace. Tears flowed down her flawless, Fashion Fair-made face. "We let you stay there because you and Mahogany were such good friends. I thought you loved to visit. I didn't know he was sexually abusing you. I'm sorry," Patty choked out.

As much as she wanted to, Royce couldn't feel any emotion over her mother's reaction, she just couldn't will herself to care. Their relationship was always contentious, and sadly, Royce carried that over into her relationship with Royale. She turned her attention to her father, who had become a mannequin.

"Daddy?"

"I trusted him and he betrayed us in the worse way. If he weren't dead, I'd kill him. But, honey, if anything, why didn't that situation not propel you into action to save your own daughter? We could have sought legal action against him, and gotten Royale help, and you. You didn't have to turn to the lifestyle you chose. You should have trusted your mother and me to take care of you. Yes, I can be overbearing and overprotective, but I have and will always love you, Royce. You didn't have to suffer in silence, but what you are doing now and what you have done is and was wrong.

"The infidelity, the lies and the secrets, all of that could and should have been avoided. If you're attempting to use your abuse to justify your current actions, well, honey, that's unacceptable.

I'm sorry a million times for the sexual abuse you encountered, and if I could go back in time to save you I would, but I don't condone your actions now. You're responsible for your actions. You should have sought therapy on your own, but instead, you chose to hurt and betray your husband and daughter. Your past pains don't negate your current actions."

She exhaled, annoyed. Did he just speak that stupidity to her? Really, so the victim was the villain? Did they not hear that she was sexually abused and then forced to abort her baby? Hello? Could she get some sympathy? Nobody ever cared about her and this right here was proof. "Please leave, I've been judged enough today and I probably lost my husband. So, leave me now," she requested, not caring how they felt or their thoughts on how she chose to live her life. It was done. Her abuse, her daughter's abuse, it was all done. Now she needed to turn her attention to taking care of her unborn baby and formulating a plan to get Grayling back.

She'd prayed to God that she and Grayling would overcome this storm. Their love was stronger than the bumps they were facing now. She had to believe that. No matter what, no matter what man she encountered, her love for Grayling never faltered. She just needed him to make her a priority and learn how to love him right. It wasn't her fault she was broken due to sexual abuse, but she was attempting to get better.

Hearing the slamming of the door was the verification she needed that her parents had taken her advice and exited the room. Good! She was exhausted and needed rest. Before she allowed her eyes to close, she called the nurse and requested that no visitors be permitted unless they were her husband, Grayling. No one else mattered. She rubbed her stomach, hoping that the child she carried belonged to Grayling. A baby would save them, so this baby had to be Grayling's. If it were Matan's child, that would ruin it all. She couldn't survive another man rejecting her. She would find a way back into Grayling's heart, or she would end him. If she couldn't have him, then no one would, including her daughter.

*   *

Matan got out of Fontaine's truck and attempted to head into the hospital. He was so focused on getting to Royce that he didn't notice the news van or the reporter until she had her microphone shoved in his face, asking him about the affair and the baby.

"Excuse me?"

"Is it true that you and reality star, Royce Chastain, have a love child? Is she leaving Bishop Grayling Chastain for you? How is Royale Chastain dealing with her ex-boyfriend being the father of her half-sibling?"

He was frozen. How had the media already gotten wind of that information when he just found out? This verified for him that Royale knew the situation. He was so dead.

"No comment," Fontaine barked, placing his hand to block the camera as he guided his friend through the small crowd and finally to the elevator.

"What was that?" Fontaine asked once they were shielded by the door.

"I don't know. Somebody leaked the story to the media, which means Royale knows. If that baby is my child, then I just lost the best woman I could ever have."

"Chill, we don't know what it is yet. Let's talk to Royce and see how far along she is. Maybe it's Bishop Grayling's child and all this worrisome talk is for nothing."

By that time, the elevator doors opened and the two made their way down to Royce's room.

"Excuse me, gentlemen, but who are you looking for?"

"Royce Chastain," Matan replied to the heavyset white nurse.

"You can't. She isn't accepting any visitors. I'm going to have to ask you to leave."

"Ma'am, supposedly, I'm one of the possible fathers of the child she is carrying and I want to see her. So, can you kindly go back to the nurses' station and let me go about my business," Matan retorted heatedly. Royce was playing too many games and he wasn't falling for it anymore. He turned around and headed back in the direction of her room with Fontaine right on his heels.

They burst into the darkened room. It was quiet, and it looked like Royce was resting. How she could relax when she single-handedly ruined his life was unknown to him. It was all starting again with her pregnancy being shared with the world. While he looked her over, nothing about her appealed to him anymore. It was all a façade that had long faded. He wondered if she tipped off the media; she would do anything to stay relevant. If that was his child, he was getting full custody because he knew she would turn into the baby mama from Hades.

He shook his head, not believing he had that thought. He went from praying the child belonged to Grayling to deciding if it were his that he would seek full custody. Wow! He padded over to the bed and called out her name. They were going to talk about this. He needed this baby to belong to Grayling and not him. He didn't want to be tied to Royce for any amount of time.

"Wake up, Royce. I know you hear me, and I'm not leaving until you tell me that's not my child you're carrying. I just found out you can get a DNA test while pregnant, so get it done."

She stirred, but didn't open her eyes. As he was about to poke her, the door opened and two security men stood there, one African American and the other Hispanic. It seemed that Nurse Piggy went and called security on him. He didn't need problems with dudes wearing uniforms, so for now, Royce was safe, but he would be back. "I just wanted to see if the baby was okay," he replied to the unanswered question.

"I understand, sir, but the patient requested no visitors. We can escort you down."

"Please do, because there is a news crew down there harassing us," Fontaine interrupted.

The men nodded and motioned for Matan and Fontaine to follow, and they did. All Matan could think about was seeing Royale. He needed to speak to her and assure her that his love for her hadn't faltered, but that he had made a mistake.

Chapter 4

After making his rounds to check on his company and his workers, Khan headed over to Mama Byse's house. He wanted to check on her and apologize again for his father's behavior. When he arrived at the house, he noticed that Keith's truck was gone, as was Kisha's car. He exited out of his truck, his signature cowboy boots digging into the gravel as he sauntered to the front door. He knocked only once and Mama Byse opened the door. She looked lovely as always. There was just something motherly about her. It had always been that way.

She stood approximately five feet six inches and had a pear shape that fit her perfectly. She wore a stylish pair of slacks and a button-down Ralph Lauren shirt. A warm smile spread across her ageless face as she reached to embrace Khan. As big as he was, he easily fell into her arms. He inhaled her scent and thought of his own mother. If Khloe Masterson was alive now, he wondered if his father would be the racist sloth he had become.

"How'd you know I needed a hug?" he asked as he pulled away and she ushered him inside.

"I'm a mom. You're as much my son as Nehemiah. I know that you're upset over what your father and his cronies did. We might not have seen them hang those nooses, but we know he was behind it. I figured you'd be back to get some things off your chest. If you need to talk to me, I'm here for you."

He nodded and followed her to the kitchen. She had a batch of double chocolate chips cookies cooling and he quickly retrieved one and put it into his mouth. It melted on his tongue and he quickly devoured two more like he hadn't eaten in ages. He sat down as she poured him a glass of chocolate milk and then she took the seat beside him.

For a moment, the two just sat in a comparable silence, neither speaking, but each understanding the other. Finally, feeling as though he had his thoughts somewhat aligned, Khan finally broke the stillness, his summer sky blue eyes gazing deeply into her dark colored terra cotta eyes. He wondered if she could read his mind. Besides the issues that Royale was facing with her own family, he had thoughts about his father's action and what he might do in the future. He was also bothered about visiting Kalid.

"Talk to me, Khan. You know this is a judgment free zone and anything we discuss remains between the two of us. I know when you grit your teeth and get that faraway look in your eyes something is bothering you. Tell me what it is so we can work through it and take it all to God in prayer."

He gave her a soft smile before replying, "Firstly, I sincerely apologize for what happened. I know he did that to get back at me, and I want you to know I'm going address his actions. I won't let him hurt you or your family when you all have been better to me than he ever has."

"Khan, you owe me no apology, what occurred is solely on your father. It is his hate and ignorance that led him to react so cowardly. I didn't yield to him when he didn't approve of my friendship with your mother and I won't yield now. You know why?" she asked.

A lifetime of emotion fast forwarded through him. His heartbeat slowly at the motherly look upon her flawless face. "No, ma'am."

"I serve a God that is greater than any man, greater than hate and has already overcome the world. My victory, worth and life belongs to Him, and nothing happens that the Father doesn't need to have happen. I know that you're upset with your father, but right now, he needs our prayers more than our wrath or revenge. I promise you that God will serve him exactly what he deserves."

He sighed. He loved Mama Byse, admired her strength and dedication to God and her family. He was thankful for her encouragement and love, but he didn't know if he had the same undying faith as she did. His father was taunting him, and yes, he wanted to be the bigger man, but if the situation advanced to more desperate attempts to get his attention, which he suspected it would, he might not be as mature about it as Mama Byse was being.

"That sounds good, and I'm really doing better about getting a closer relationship with God. Royale even has me doing my quiet time. However, I'm not as mature in my walk as you and she are, nor have I been baptized yet. So, if Pops comes again, I may not react in love and understanding. Sometimes you have to go a little deeper and my father has hated too long to understand love," Khan explained.

"No one is ever a lost cause until their death bed, and even then, God can save a sincere heart. Just give prayer a try and make sure you come to Sunday service and Bible Study if you can," she replied with motherly affection, resting her ochre-tone freckle-laced hand on top of his. Again, it crossed his mind why something like skin tone divided people to the point that they wanted to kill another for being a darker shade, and yet his father and his other racist friends loved sunbathing and tanning to darken their skin. It baffled him as to why they hated others for their God-given melanin. There was no logic for such rancor.

"Yes, ma'am, I'll try. You have my word," he assured her.

She nodded.

"There's something else."

"I know. Let me guess, it has to do with Royale."

She always amazed him with how astute she was. "Right. I guess that you've noticed how close the two of us have become. I'm falling fast for her, which is another reason why I need to resolve this issue with my father. She is facing some trials as well. Earlier, I received a phone call from Royale, and she was upset.

"After I leave here, I'm headed to Virginia to be with her," he told her, then took a deep breath before continuing. Without looking at her, he knew that she was wondering what was going on. "So, I don't know how much you know about Royale and her family, but when she returned home, she found out her mother was pregnant with Matan's child, or at least that is the suspicion. I guess it could possibly be her father's child as well."

He heard the sharp intake of breath and looked up to see that Kisha had entered the kitchen with a stunned look on her face. "What the what?" she exclaimed, shocked.

"Her mother is pregnant. I think it's going to be a news story, considering who they are. I need to see her, but I wanted to check in on Mama Byse before I left. Nehemiah is going to look after things, but my cousin has to fly back to Texas to deal with some issues for his client." Then he turned his attention back to Mama Byse.

"I have to head out now, but I'll be in contact. Let me know if the old man starts anything else. Once I'm calmer, I'll contact him, but until then, pray for us all. I really want to be the man you think I am. I really want to let God lead, and me follow, but sometimes, I can get impatient."

"I'll pray, and so will you. Always pray first and then react. Don't worry about us. Keith will be home for a while and I'm fine. You just take care of Royale and let her know we love her and have her in our prayers."

"Yes, ma'am," he replied, then got up and hugged her before turning his attention to Kisha and embracing her as well.

"I want to come."

"Kisha, let me check on her first, then I'll let you know. Besides, she's coming back with me on Friday."

She pouted, which would normally allow her to get her way, but he really wanted to spend time with Royale alone and get to know her family. He knew that Kisha understood that. She nodded her acquiesce and he exited the house and headed to his truck. Taking a deep breath, he exhaled a smile. He was going to see Royale, even though he didn't want it to be under such circumstances, the idea of seeing her again made all his troubles seem tiny. He had it bad for her.

*　*

It was done, and it was executed well, Ronald thought to himself as a devilish smile stretched across his face. Now all he had to do was wait. Some of his old buddies called and informed him that the boy had gone to the police. He knew it was coming. He knew Khan would reach out. He was sure that his son knew or at least suspected that he was behind the threat that happened at the Byse's home as well as the burning of his business. He needed to get Khan's attention and let him know that he meant business. He was done looking like a fool for his son. If that didn't bring Khan back to his senses, he had much more planned.

"Ron, your son is on the move. He went to the police station, then to his mother's grave, and after that, he headed to the Byse residence. I'm having him tailed and it seems he's leaving the state," Hoss interrupted.

That had Ronald perplexed. Where was his son going exactly? He sighed and rolled his eyes. "Tell whomever you have following him to keep me updated on where he is going. I'd like a full report."

Hoss nodded. "You think we need to turn up the heat? The boys in Tennessee and Kentucky are itching to get into some fun. I do like the smell of burning wood."

"Let's see what he does first."

"Right, well, let's get a drink."

"Yeah, I can do a beer." It was the last thing he needed per his doctor. His traitorous body was turning against him, but he'd deal with that later.

*　*

Royale crossed her long, thick, even-toned legs and let out a low hiss. She was annoyed, upset, hurt and mentally fatigued. The day had worn her out and she couldn't wait for Khan to arrive. He'd take the pressure away because it was all mounting and she felt like she would explode. Sadly, the news media had already caught wind of the fact that her vessel was pregnant. They even caught Matan entering the hospital. She couldn't lie, that stung a little bit. She wasn't sure why and wasn't prepared to unpack and dissect those emotions. After he sent her the emotional email, she thought he had learned his lesson, but there he was, visiting Royce.

Royale looked over at her father, who seemed just as drained and detached. She couldn't stand seeing his face drawn in agony due to Royce's deceit. She knew his heart was breaking and that was breaking her own heart. Her father, the man who preached about moving mountains and having the faith of a mustard seed, now seemed smaller, less relaxed and full of worry and discontent. For the first time in her life, she wasn't sure what words to speak to ease the terrible, scarring pain attacking not just his physical, but his mental and spiritual.

He said all the right things at the late-night church meeting, reminding the flock that even though he wouldn't be in the forefront, he was still there for them. He explained that he needed to take the time to work on his family and heal. She'd admired him for standing up and answering invasive questions and silencing fears, but at the end of the day, her father was only human. Though they were surrounded by family, his sister, Antwon, her grandparents and Rina, she knew he appreciated the support as she did. However, watching the media rehash it all was like ripping stitches from an unhealed surgical wound. Royce had punctured Grayling's soul and left him to bleed out spiritually. Royale wasn't going to allow her father to go out like that. She would find a way to help him heal, as well as herself. One way to do that was to get this situation off the evening news.

That was what people failed to understand. In their thirst to see another backslide and hunger to watch the suffering of a celebrity family, they somehow dehumanize the innocent, all to have an excuse not to deal with their own problems. Honestly, if Royale knew who sold them out, she would have explained to them just how much unnecessary agony they put on her family. She, like her father, was starting to regret ever being part of the reality show. What they were living now was almost too much to bear. Add in the cameras and the opinions of ignorant people who had no clue about their current situation, it was agonizing. They wanted a story, and she knew she and her father needed to control said story, and the best way to do that was to reach out to Trinity. She was a Christian talk show host with her own show called *Answering the Call with Trinity Hall*. If they could control the narrative, then maybe that would take some of the pressure off her father.

Unable to take her father's sorrowful look any longer, she excused herself and walked to her bedroom with Rina hot on her heels. Royale needed some sister talk about a lot of things. She wanted to share with Rina all that had occurred in West Virginia without the family knowing. If they knew that she met a new guy and that Khan's father was a racist, then they would end the relationship even before it started.

"You okay, sis?" Rina asked, worry painted onto her creamy, butterscotch skin, her green eyes darkened by the allegations and accusations the media was spreading about their family.

Fighting back tears of exhaustion, Royale plopped down at the edge of her bed and smiled at Rina. It wasn't a comforting smile, more of a survival smile. "There are a billion thoughts circulating in my head, and I don't even know where to start. I'm extremely concerned about Daddy. He doesn't deserve this. He's a God-fearing man, who has taken on the burden of others, loved with a faith that I've prayed to have and been faithful to an unfaithful woman. She cares more about herself and manipulating others to ever be a good wife or mother.

"Now our name is being dragged through the mud again because she doesn't know who impregnated her. Instead of accepting her wrongs and seeking to make amends, she blames it on everybody else. I'm so mad, Rina. I'm so livid and completely done with her excuses that I could scream," Royale confessed, irritated. She was also pissed with herself for allowing Royce to upset her. After leaving the hospital and waiting for her father to return to the truck, she mentally chastised herself for going low and not high. She would pray about it all and seek God's guidance on how to proceed. Even though Royce hurt her deeply, she was still her vessel, and she needed to apologize for speaking so harshly to her. Clearing her head, she looked at Rina who had a contemplative look on her face, willing her to understand where she was coming from, and she did.

"I know, Royale. I know how it feels when a parent betrays your trust. It's like an unhealable wound that festers and erupts like a volcano at will. You never know what will trigger it or how long the pain will last. My bio-father hasn't been in my life for years, but certain smells, phrases, even my mother's facial expressions, can bring back a memory and I feel like I'm there again.

"At the end of the day, God is greater than every fear, problem, or worry. We're not children anymore, Royale. We know where to go for comfort, we know that God has never and will never forsake us, and lastly, we know we belong to Him. He's the kind of Father that never leaves His children behind. When you feel despair or discouraged, pray. Pray with intention and with un-shakable faith and know that He hears our every cry and an-swers our prayers on time."

Royale and Rina had tears glistening in their eyes. A warm smile crossed Royale's face; her little cousin was growing up and had grown wise. "Young grasshopper, when did you learn to drop that Godly wisdom?" she teased as she widened her arms for Rina to embrace her.

Rina smiled and leaned into her, accepting her embrace. "I have had many years to learn from my cousin slash sister. Now, how about we change the subject to something lighter. Let's talk about something that makes you smile," Rina suggested as she pulled away.

Royale gave her a questionable look as if she hadn't already inferred the meaning of her cousin's statement. She knew Rina wanted to know about all things Khan, and who was she kidding because she wanted to share. Khan had swept her off her feet in one day.

"Don't give me that look like I'm speaking a foreign language. You know I'm talking about Khan. With everything that has been occurring recently, I've failed at my duties to gain as much information about him as possible. The night I was supposed to do my intense internet search, Marc pulled that stunt on me. So, spill all the tea on him."

Royale shook her head at how giddy Rina was and couldn't help but guffaw. It was a genuine laugh that was full and hearty. She wanted to tell Rina how she felt about Khan, however, parts of her felt guilty for feeling happiness at what was growing between herself and Khan when her family was falling apart. Licking her lips, she stopped laughing and gave Rina a serious stare. "Do you think I'm selfish for meeting a new guy and being happy when there's so much anguish and malevolence around here?"

Rina's face frowned as she contemplated Royale's question. "No. Why should you put your happiness on hold because of the actions of another person? You deserve to enjoy life and to move on, and if this guy brings you joy, then I'm happy for you. Tell me it all over again, how you met and everything. I need to live vicariously through you since guys still make me nervous."

Royale's eyes glowed in delight. "Well, first off, you're going to get to meet him in the flesh since he might be here early in the morning. I told him all about the happenings of the day."

"Wow, you feel that comfortable with him?" she queried, surprised.

"Yes. It was instantaneous. My tire blew out, he arrived, all six feet four inches—give or take—of him, walking with that Stetson Man swagger and offering to change my tire. He was so fine that I was momentarily speechless. He probably thought I was a little on the slow side. Anyway, he was extremely polite and such a gentleman. He told me to call him if I needed more assistance, and then the next day, he's sitting in the kitchen at the Byse's house and I'm all fangirl when he starts talking to me. Kisha sold me up the river, calling me out because I told her I met a sexy cowboy, and of course, that was him. After that, we started spending every day together and talking on the phone all through the night. His voice just gives me peace of mind. There's something magnetic about his vocal cadence."

"How dreamy. Do you have pictures? I need to see this brotha."

Royale grinned as she recalled the impromptu photo session she had when they went hiking. He looked so handsome. She quickly pulled out her iPhone and let Rina browse through the photos. She watched Rina's facial expression and noticed how the excitement slowly faded, prompting Royale to ask what was the matter.

Rina glanced up at her, her face red and eyes alarmed. She looked as if she were having an allergic reaction. "Rina, what is it? Are you viewing pictures of Khan or someone else?" She was sure she deleted all the pictures of Matan.

"He's a white guy? I thought he was a brotha," she questioned, her normally soft green eyes glowed with disquietude, causing Royale to feel defensive and anxious.

Tilting her head to the right, and exhaling the anxiousness that began to eat at her core, she slowly looked at Rina and carefully replied, "No. I thought I told you that, and even if I didn't, why does it matter?" She never knew Rina to care about skin color before since she was bi-racial and dealt with people making fun of her because of it.

"So, he's white and he's from West Virginia, like my bio-father," she stated, alarmed. Her skin began to turn red as she spoke. There was tension in her shoulders and Royale could see that it really bothered her that Khan was Caucasian.

For a moment, Royale was perplexed, unable to follow Rina's train of thought. Then it slapped Royale in the face and she understood where Rina was coming from. Somehow, Rina was connecting the fact that because Khan was white and from West Virginia that he was like Strom Evans, Rina's abusive, biological father, who actually had another family in West Virginia. However, Khan wasn't abusive and he sure was nothing like Strom Evans. "Czarina Gail," she stated, calling her by her entire name. "Khan is nothing like him. Yes, they have skin color and location in common, but Khan's not abusive and he wouldn't hurt me in that way. He sure doesn't have a whole family tucked away in another state." Of course, that wasn't to say his father wouldn't be an issue, but she didn't want to bring that up with Rina. She hadn't even told her about the epic run-in she had with Everleigh.

"You don't know him that well. Momma said when she first met Strom, he was this wonderful, God-fearing man who treated her like she was the only person in the world. He doted on her and was devoted to her. That was until he showed the true devil that he is. He flipped, even you've seen what he can do. He freaking pistol whipped you. Who is to say that this Khan isn't the same?" she argued. "I mean, have you even met his family? Who are they, what do they do? I just don't have a good feeling about this," Rina replied while she started to type in Khan Masterson into a search engine.

"What are you doing?" Royale asked.

"I'm doing an internet search like I meant to do before."

"Rina, that's not necessary."

"Yes, it is," she argued.

"It won't change anything. Khan has nothing to hide from me. I know his past as he knows mine. Trust me, Rina."

"Sis, I can't. Remember Matan? I wasn't a fan of his either, but you said trust me, Rina, and I did. Now, look at the mess we're in because of him and Aunt Royce. Sorry, chica, but when it comes to men, you don't do enough undercover work."

That hurt her feelings a little bit. She didn't know that Rina felt that way. "Wow, Rina. I had no idea you thought so lowly of me," she replied, her voice cracking.

Rina stopped typing and glanced up at Royale and immediately apologized. "I didn't mean it like that. I have the highest respect for you. What I mean is our family usually gets dumped on; it happened with my mom, your dad, and you. The only reason I haven't been heartbroken by a man is because I avoid relationships. I admire the fact that you can mend your heart and give love a try again, but I want you safe and with a man who is worthy of your love and good heart."

"Khan is. I promise. He's had it hard too. His mother was murdered in front of him, the man accused and convicted of it is getting a new trial, his father is a member of the Christian Identity and hates everyone who isn't white. Additionally, before I left, his father burned his business because Khan refused to become part of or accept the philosophy of the Klan and Christian Identity. I respect him and love him even more for standing up for his beliefs knowing that he will ultimately lose his father, the only other living parent he has. Yes, I am all in with him and I have no reservations about his feelings for me. He won't break my heart and I won't break his heart," she passionately expressed, forgetting all about not sharing that information with Rina.

"Whoa, wait a minute. You're saying that you love him? A man you just met whose father is associated with domestic terrorists that hate us and thinks a person like me is an abomination. Oh, mercy, don't tell the parents or the General any of this," she advised as she wiped sweat from her brow. "I need to meet this Khan, and if I get any bad vibes, he's out."

"Czarina."

"Nope, don't Czarina me, this is dangerous. Are you even listening to yourself? You love a man whose father is associated with racist terrorist and you see nothing wrong with that? It's because you're emotional after everything that has happened, and you're not thinking clearly. He could be taking advantage of you. The Klan kills people. They could hurt you, and then what? I don't know what kind of love you think you're feeling, but I strongly suggest you slow it down to a snail's pace. It's too soon to be talking about love."

Before Royale could reply, her cell started ringing. It was Khan, and she smiled before answering.

"Hey, Khan, are you almost here?" she asked, ignoring the O that Rina's lips had formed. She knew Rina was in her feelings about how Royale felt about Khan, but she didn't care. Royale knew her heart and she wasn't ashamed to have fallen so quickly for a man who treated her better in an hour than Matan had in their entire relationship.

"Yes, I was going to head to a hotel and come see you in the morning."

"Nonsense, Khan, come to my house. We have an entire basement that has been remodeled into an apartment. You can stay there; meet my family and I'll show you around Virginia and DC. Please say you'll stay."

"You know I can't say no to you. I'll be there in a bit."

"Okay, see you then," she replied, ignoring the gawking stare Rina was giving her.

*   *

Matan sat on his bed, head embedded in his hands, head pounding and heart thumping irregularly. His cell had been ringing nonstop and he ignored all calls. His mother had called him, but he didn't want to speak to her because a part of him believed she had contacted the media. He wanted to reach out to Royale. When he was stressed like this and unable to think clearly, she was always there with a verse and a prayer. He needed that more than anything, but he knew she wasn't ready. He wasn't even sure if he were ready. He sighed.

Against his better judgment, he grabbed his keys. He needed to see her. He needed her to hear his apology and his plea for a second chance.

"Yo, where are you heading out to? I thought you wanted to stay in to avoid the media," Fontaine called out, pushing his glasses back up.

"I'll be back. I just need to take a drive to clear my mind."

"Are you sure? You've been a little off since we left the hospital. I don't want you doing anything dumb. Just chill out for the night, man."

"I appreciate you looking out, but I really need some alone time. I'm cool. You have my word that I won't do anything foolish or illegal. I'm chill."

Fontaine shook his head, but it was obvious that Matan didn't want advice. He already had in his mind what he wanted to do. Fontaine watched worriedly as his friend exited out their shared apartment.

Matan hopped into his car and drove toward Royale's and Grayling's home. He didn't know if she was there or at Gwendolyn's house, but he didn't care, he'd go to both. He was desperate to talk to Royale before he lost her for good. He just couldn't lose her. He could give her time to get over his infidelity, but there was no way he could live without her. He needed her to understand that, which was why he needed the child that Royce was carrying to be Grayling's and not his.

Chapter 5

Grayling and his father-in-law, Eli, fondly called the General, sat in Grayling's study, smoking Cuban cigars, both intensely embedded in their own thoughts. Grayling needed to clear his mind because he was flabbergasted by how the media had discovered that his wife was pregnant. He was beginning to think that either Marc or his wife tipped off the media. He wasn't sure, however, how else could it have happened? That was what his mind was toying with when Eli suggested they go into Grayling's study once the girls went to Royale's bedroom.

His family was crumbling right before his eyes and right when he thought he had a handle on the issues threatening to derail his family, another problem popped up. Like now. Something else was brewing because the entire time Patty and the General had been in his home, he felt the tension. Something was on both their minds, but neither had said anything and he wondered if the General was going to inform him of what was going on.

Finally, the General let out a long sigh and then turned his attention to Grayling. The General's normal authoritative, assured eyes showcased a weakness tonight. Something was bothering him, and Grayling assumed he would find out right now. "Son, I need to tell you something. I don't know how you're going to feel about it, but it'll possibly give you some insight as to why Royce has acted out like this. Why she has jeopardized her marriage, family, and character."

Grayling put the cigar down and ran his hands down his face. He had no idea what was about to come out of the General's mouth, but he really couldn't care less about Royce's excuses. She had made a total mess and mockery of God, her family and the man who loved her. He wasn't trying to be cruel or vindictive, but he was sick of hearing her name. He was tired of reliving the pain and attempting to understand why she did what she did. It hurt too much to continue to speak on it and now there was an unborn child in the middle. It sickened him to his core. He lifted his head up and matched the General's stare before saying, "I don't want to know."

The General shook his head. His dark, imposing eyes snapped at Grayling. He was instantly back to himself. "You don't have a choice. I know you're upset, embarrassed and hurt, but you need to hear this. When Patty and I went to confront Royce, she dropped a bomb, and before you say it is part of her manipulation, I called and verified the story. When Royce was twelve, she started being molested by her godfather, my best friend, and personal attorney, Lance Kirkland. She told me that from the age of twelve to almost seventeen he raped her. Then she got pregnant at sixteen and he forced her to have an abortion. She suffered this abuse, this trauma, without her mother or me to help her. It all happened during the the 70s. It was a different time back then and I guess she felt like she had to keep it a secret. I think that's what has caused her sexual addiction and egotistical behavior. I'm no therapist, but I would assume that's the reasoning.

"Now, before you comment, I told her that her abuse doesn't excuse her actions. I also told her that the affairs, and allowing Larry to fondle her daughter was wrong. She kicked us out after that. After I had a moment to reflect and calm myself, I reached out to Lance's daughter, Mahogany, and she told me what she knew. Her deceased father had an inappropriate relationship with my daughter and forced her to have an abortion, the latter she discovered later. She always thought Royce had a miscarriage. Apparently, her father kept detailed notes in his journal, which she discovered upon his death."

Grayling didn't know what to think, and the pounding headache that finally stopped was back in full force. The devil was shooting all his fiery darts, and every dart was making contact. He wasn't built to sustain this constant barrage of spiritual assaults. It was like having a gong being repeatedly hit. He felt light headed. He dropped his head in his hands and started practicing his yoga breathing, calming himself. He thought of Erica Campbell's song "Help", and God knows he needed all of God's help. He opened his eyes once more, showcasing just how much this ordeal had taken from him. He was mentally exhausted.

"Eli, I don't know what I'm supposed to do with that information. I told her it was over after I found out she forced Royale to keep the secrets from me. Secrets that I believe are the cause of her anxiety attacks. That should be enough for me to let her go, but even as I told her that I was done, I still love her. I love my wife, Eli, but I don't trust her. I don't think I ever will. How can I stay married to a woman when I don't trust her with my heart? How can I be a husband to a wife who has violated my trust and our vows?

"My heart goes out to her to have been raped by her godfather, and then to get pregnant and forced to kill her own child, but," he paused for a second, his eyes going skyward as he tried to comprehend the actions of Royce. Failing to do so, he let out a sigh, shook his pounding head and glared back at his father-in-law. "I wonder why she put Royale in that same situation. She's not prepared to be a wife or mother and I can't force her to be. My plan isn't changing. I'm still packing her bags and shipping them to you. When she's discharged from her therapy program, she can't come back here. I'll not lose my daughter to gain my wife nor will I lose myself for her. I've said it before and I mean it. I'll pray for her and love her at a distance, but we can't remain," Grayling replied, sitting up straight, his muscled legs spreading in a V-shape, eyes focused on the General. Grayling loathed admitting that, but for him, love didn't just leave. At the same time, love wasn't always enough.

The General nodded his understanding before speaking. "I respect that, Grayling, I do. I know you and Royale are severely scarred by Royce's repulsive actions. Honestly, I can't tell you what to do, but I know you are a man of God. Before you make any drastic decisions, please seek God's counsel and don't react on your own emotions or understanding." He stopped for a moment. Grayling assumed it was equally as hard for him, but no matter what Royce did, the General was her father and loved her unconditionally. He understood the General's need to protect his daughter, and he hoped the General understood his need to protect Royale. He respectfully listened to the General as he continued speaking, but he was sure he wouldn't change his mind about Royce.

"Royce needs help, like serious trauma-focused help. She's in her late 40s and has been keeping that secret since she was twelve. I can't imagine how that screwed up her mind. I know my daughter loves you. She's made some ignorant choices that make me question her sanity, but knowing what she has survived, I sort of understand. I hope you will too."

"I hear you." That was all he could manage. He needed to be in his warrior room praying because this was just an overload of emotion and he couldn't compartmentalize.

"One more thing."

Grayling groaned. What else could there possibly be now? "Okay," he replied dryly, his molasses skin paling at the thought of more bombshells. Lord knows when it rains, it pours, but he felt like he was in a tsunami.

"I found Leering Larry. Actually, he's Larry Eland Audubon, lived in Lynchburg, VA, age fifty, unmarried and childless. Anyway, he's currently under the supervision of some of my Army Ranger friends, hence why I said lived in Lynchburg. Now, I know you're a saved man who no longer participates in street justice, but if you need to blow off some steam..."

Grayling chuckled. The General's confession lightened up the dark mood that had settled between the pair. He sure appreciated the General's tenacity because that was fast. The General was something else. Just as he was about to reply, he was interrupted by the doorbell ringing. Who would be ringing his doorbell at his hour? They got their answer quickly as they exited the study.

There before them was Matan. He looked unkempt, as if he hadn't had rest or time to bathe. To Grayling's shock, Royale stood stiffly glaring at a worn Matan. Her facial features were hard and angry, eyes locked on him like a predatory animal seeking to end her prey. That was a surprise to him. He knew the two hadn't spoken or seen each other since the run-in at Starbucks and he prayed Matan wasn't here to start another circus.

"What are you doing at my home?" Royale interrogated, a look of disdain and pure terror dressed her normally beautiful, glowing face. Instantly, hearing the uncertainty and wavering of his daughter's voice caused Grayling and the General to shift into warrior mode. The pair stalked toward the entrance hall like a pair of lions stalking their territory, looking fierce and ready for battle. "Matan, my granddaughter asked you a question. Answer it, now!" the General bellowed.

Matan's eyes never left Royale's as he answered the demanding question of the General. "I needed to speak to Royale and Bishop Grayling. I wanted to apologize to her as well as to you, Bishop Grayling. I need to ask you both for your forgiveness. I miss my friend and confidant, and I miss my mentor. What I did to you both was horrible and wrong. I'm so sorry for the trespasses I committed against you both," he asserted, eyes red from rubbing them constantly to hold hostage the tears that wanted to fall.

Grayling stopped short. He hadn't expected Matan to sound so sincere or to accept responsibility for his actions. It tugged at his heart and he could hear God speaking to him. He was hurt by Matan's actions, but he wasn't angry with him, at least not anymore. Honestly, he felt sorry for him. The more he learned about the devious deeds of his wife, the more he felt like Matan might have been a victim also. Matan's plea and heartfelt apology broke down Grayling's defenses. "Matan, come on and have a seat. God sent you here for a reason. There's been enough finger pointing, yelling, and resentment. Let's try to heal," he offered, knowing it was God speaking through him.

"Daddy?" Royale pouted.

"Sweetheart, we have to treat people like God treats us, not the way people treat us. If we treat men with the same malevolence that is used against us, then we are no better than the world. The Lord expects us as His children to be the light and the salt of the world. I understand your agony, but right now, Matan needs our prayer and a haven, and we can offer both. If his presence is too much for you, then you can excuse yourself, but I won't turn him away and you won't treat him unkindly," Grayling replied, seemingly shocking everyone, including Matan.

Grayling only wished he had that same compassion for his wife. In time, he would, he hoped, but for now, that was too much, so he understood if his daughter wasn't ready to speak to Matan. Betrayal always felt worse when loved ones were the people committing the actions.

"Daddy, I just...I have..." Before she finished her sentence, another voice was added to the conversation.

"Royale, I'm here," Khan replied with a big smile, reaching for her hand.

The world stopped turning. It was quieter than a library. Everyone stood stock-still, bodies rigid and unflinching, eyes staring at the uninvited stranger, mouths in various stages of being wide open to gaping like oxygen-deprived fish. Before them stood an unknown Caucasian male, taller than both Grayling and the General. He sported long, blond hair, summer blue eyes, tanned skin and the beginnings of a beard. Before anyone could speak, Royale had wrapped her arms around the large-muscled man, who returned the gesture. It was as if they had forgotten they weren't alone.

Astoundingly, Grayling noted, Royale acted as if the first five minutes had never occurred. Her reaction was a complete one-eighty. Her once angry face was now smooth, calm, glowing with admiration and joy. Her body language was free and inviting.

This piqued Grayling's interest because he didn't know this stranger, yet his daughter seemed extremely relaxed and overly welcoming to the newest addition. The entire room remained frozen into place, except for the stranger and Royale. It was on the tip of Grayling's tongue to interrogate this stranger, but the other family members arrived right then. He assumed they had taken refuge in the kitchen and out of curiosity, came to see what was happening.

"Royale, sweetheart, who is this fine, tall glass of whole milk?" Patty asked, looking like she had been deep in the cups, and not milk. Her normally well-groomed locks were out of place, and her gait was off. She'd been in the wine or the liquor cabinet because her brilliant chocolate diamond eyes were dull, sad and watery. Patty never looked like that.

Grayling suspected the demure, unkempt appearance of Patty had to do with the confession that Royce had made about being sexually assaulted for years. If he were honest, it greatly impacted him as well, but for now, he was focused on the two guests; Matan and the strange man being way too familiar and touchy with his daughter. He cleared his throat, folded his arms and waited for his daughter to reply. He sure hoped his daughter wasn't jumping into another relationship so quickly after Matan. Her heart still hadn't healed from the first heartbreak, and he was sure she needed closure and not to start a new relationship.

"Harpo, who dis white man?" Antwon asked, breaking the tension in the room. Grayling could only shake his head but was thankful for the moment of comic relief. He kept an eye on Matan, who looked like he was about to lose his mind. He prayed to God he hadn't made a mistake by welcoming Matan into his home.

"Sorry everyone for my lack of manners, I was just so excited that he finally arrived. This is Khan Masterson. We met in West Virginia while I was visiting Kisha and her family. Khan rescued me when I ran off the road. He's also Nehemiah Byse's best friend. Anyway, we met, we clicked and he's here because I needed his support after everything that has occurred today." Then, she turned to Khan. "Khan, that's the General, he's my maternal grandfather, that beautiful lady there is my grandmother, Patty Royce, beside the General is my father, Bishop Grayling, and that's his sister, Ma Gwendolyn, and beside her is Antwon, my godfather. Rina is still upstairs."

"It's nice to finally put the faces and names together. It's a pleasure to meet you all. I'm sorry for arriving this late, but I had to travel from West Virginia as you know," Khan replied politely.

Grayling nodded a salutation, but he wasn't at all impressed with the man who stood before him. He didn't like how his daughter was reacting to this young man. She had her entire family for support, why did she need this unknown? Who was he, who was his family, was he a plant for the media, and was he looking for his fifteen minutes of fame? He vetted people thoroughly before he allowed anyone to enter his home, and it caused him concern that his daughter, who had never mentioned a Khan Masterson to him, now had said man in their home. Not only that, but she failed to introduce him to Matan and that made him wonder if this Khan was the jealous type.

"Well, you all, I'm going to take Khan down to the basement apartment so he can get settled and get some sleep. It's been a long journey for him," Royale quipped.

"Hold up, Royale. I came here, humble and apologetic for the pain I caused when I betrayed your trust. Now you are dating another man like all those years I put in meant nothing," Matan chafed.

"Cool your overheated jets, Matan. If you continue to speak out of turn to my goddaughter, I'ma bless you with David and Samson," he warned, showing his fists at Matan.

"Antwon, stop that," Gwendolyn admonished, placing her smaller hand atop his large ones in warning. He dropped them at her request, but his face was still menacing.

"Wait, you're Matan?" Khan questioned, making everyone pause and glare at him. No one was sure of how this would play out. Khan didn't waver in speech and remained cucumber cool as he glared right into Matan's eyes, even though a few feet separated them. "Well, I offer you my thanks. Royale is in excellent hands now," Khan professed as he wrapped his arms around Royale.

Matan's body bulked up, his eyes challenging Khan. The tension had risen and everyone could feel it. Though the two were apart, it felt like they were face to face.

"Oh, simmer down, boys," Patty hiccupped out.

"Whatever, I don't need this," Matan fumed as he heatedly trotted out the door, not bothering to close it.

Before Grayling could comment, Royale and her new beau ambled through the small crowd and headed downstairs towards the basement, seemingly as if nothing had occurred.

"What the heck just happened?" the General asked, unable to comprehend what he had just witnessed. "For me, this Khan could be another Strom Evans, and what was all that yakking Matan just did? He needs his butt beat."

Before anyone could speculate or answer the question, Rina came jogging down the stairs after hearing loud voices. She had completely missed the introduction of Khan Masterson and the arrival and departure of Matan. Grayling's eyes shot up as she entered the family room. "Rina, sweetheart, who is Khan Masterson, and why is he in our home?"

Grayling noticed how Rina looked around the room as she realized everyone expected her to have an answer. The girls were close and he knew neither liked the idea of telling on the other.

Finally, she took a deep breath and answered, "Dad, he's the guy she met in West Virginia. I didn't know he was white until just a moment ago. I never got a chance to do an internet search on him, so I didn't know. Anyway, I told Royale how I felt about it, you know, to be careful and to make sure she wasn't rebounding, but she's completely captivated by him. Honestly, that worries me."

"Bump an internet search, I'm doing a full NSA, FBI, Homeland Security background check on him and his entire family.

Grayling, you need to talk to my granddaughter; she's acting like she's grown and pays all the bills. Her spoiled behind don't pay anything. I know she's conflicted and confused because of her mother, but she just brought a stranger to stay in the house, one that comes from the same place as Strom Evans. I won't have a replay," he hissed, shaking his head. "I mean, who does that? Who meets a man on Monday and brings him home on Tuesday? You know she's not too grown for me to put across my lap. Almost grown folks need butt whippings too," the General concluded.

"Hush up and calm down, Eli. My goodness, have a little faith in our granddaughter. Royale is and has always been responsible. I trust her judgment. FYI, we met like that, so don't go acting brand new like love at first sight is unheard of. Oh, and if you attempt to put a hand on her, you'll be the one singing soprano. Besides, it didn't work on Royce, why do you think it would work on Royale?" Patty cuttingly defended.

"Look here, soul sista, you've been in the liquor, so your opinion is invalid until you sober up!" he snapped.

Gwendolyn dropped her head and let out a giggle and Grayling's eyes widened at his father-in-law chastising his mother-in-law. The two of them rarely disagreed in public, it was one of their rules, so to witness this was astounding.

"Eli, I'm not drunk. I'm just in a state of shock about what happened to our daughter right under our nose and by a man we trusted. Don't even start with me right now, it won't end well for you," she warned.

Sensing that the situation was about to blow to epic proportion, Grayling attempted to be the voice of reason. "Okay, everyone, just take a few deep breaths and relax, we're all exhausted and need some rest. Eli and Patty, y'all can have the master bedroom. It's been a long night and late morning, so head on to bed. Rina, you look like you could use some sleep too. I'll wait on Royale," he told them before turning to his sister and Antwon. He motioned for them to follow him to the kitchen.

"I wanted to talk to you both earlier, but with everything that has been happening, I haven't had the time."

"What's on your mind?" Gwendolyn asked, concerned.

"Nothing bad, I just wanted to let you both know that you can stop pretending. I know that you and Antwon have been seeing each other. I'm glad. You both deserve happiness and love," he told them and then directed his attention to Antwon. "I love you like a brother, but if you hurt her, I'll forget our friendship and take it back to the old days."

"You've known this entire time?" Gwendolyn queried, shocked.

"I've known for a while now. I don't know if the girls know because I haven't told them, but if they are as perceptive and as intuitive as I think, then they most likely know as well and just haven't commented on it."

"G, you know I would never disrespect your sister or anybody in this family. I love her, and I want to marry her."

Grayling didn't miss the huge smile that graced his sister's face. He winked at her. "Whenever y'all are ready, I'll be more than happy to do the ceremony."

"Thanks. I guess we better get going," Antwon replied as he wrapped his arm protectively around Gwendolyn. "Oh, and tomorrow, me, you and the General need to take the Jolly Green Giant out so we can get to know him better."

"You better believe it," Grayling cosigned and the trio sauntered toward the door. As soon as he said goodnight to his sister and best friend, he heard his daughter's footfalls.

"Daddy."

"Royale, we need to have a conversation right now. I'm not angry, but we are amid a storm and you bring an unknown into this drama, who I know nothing about, and that concerns me greatly."

"Daddy, I know. I should've told you, but I haven't had the time with the announcement that I have a sibling on the way. The media is hounding us again, and I just needed comfort. I know, Rina probably told you that I love him and it's not puppy love, lust or confusion. All I know is I went to West Virginia to breathe and I found him. He gets me. He doesn't care about the drama, or who I am, all he cares about is me. I'm just Royale Makeda Chastain, and I like that. He's nothing like Matan, nor am I using him to get over Matan. I admit I was wrong to invite him to stay without your consent, but he's my friend and I care immensely for him as he does me."

That wasn't what he thought she would say and he still had his doubts, but her passionate plea was enough to settle the talk for later. Maybe he was becoming soft in his old age, but he didn't have the energy to undertake a serious conversation. "I respect your feelings. It's late, so we'll table this for later. Right now, you need to go to bed. It's been a long day. I'm weary. Your grandparents are staying the night, as is Rina. Your aunt and Godfather have left."

She nodded. "Night, Daddy, and I'm sorry about how I introduced Khan to you."

"It's okay. Go get some rest." He watched her go, and then he collapsed on the sofa. His mind was busy as thoughts ran rampant. All he thought about was his wife's deception, the General finding Larry, his daughter falling for a man named Khan and that Strom Evans wanted to reunite with Rina.

Lastly, Matan. That boy needed somebody, but he wasn't sure if he was the right someone. His head was pounding, and at this rate, even though he was taxed physically, mentally and spiritually, he could not rest, so he prayed. At first, his prayer was just tears because that was all he had the strength to form, but he knew that God heard his cry and could decipher the words his vocal chords couldn't form, and slowly, the rest he so desperately sought came as did the verses Colossians 1:13. *He has delivered us from the power of darkness and conveyed us into the kingdom of the Son of His love.* And Isaiah 61:3, *To console those who mourn in Zion, To give them beauty for ashes, The oil of joy for mourning, The garment of praise for the spirit of heaviness; That they may be called trees of righteousness, a planting of the Lord, that He may be glorified.* The scriptures serenaded him to a peaceful slumber. It would be all right. God was in charge and there was nothing too big for the Great I AM.

Chapter 6

Nina Byse sat down with Kalid and let out a sigh of contentment. She was beyond overjoyed that he was getting a new trial, though she wanted the entire conviction to be overthrown and him a free man because he had broken no law and committed no crime. Patiently, he waited. He waited for nearly fifteen years for this moment, and through those years, she prayed for him.

Kalid was family. He was her husband's cousin and he was the main reason why she did a weekly ministry at the prison. She wanted to ensure his safety and keep an eye on him because she knew just how vicious Ronald could and would be. Kalid offered her a soft smile, reminding her of her husband. Keith and Kalid both shared silky, curly hair, soft butter-stained skin and deep hazel eyes that were warm and welcoming. Where her husband was stocky and average in height, Kalid was thinly muscled like a basketball player and just as tall.

Khan had no idea that she even knew Kalid, but Ronald did, which only added to the reasons why he detested her so much. Ronald tended to blame everyone else for his wife's death but refused to accept his blame in what happened. She was more than ready for the entire truth to be told, but it wasn't her place or her story to tell.

"What's on your mind, Nina? Something happened?"

"Ronald is starting up again. He hung several scarecrows on a tree in the yard to remind me of my place, then he set his own son's business on fire. I can't say for sure, but I feel like I'm being followed. I just wanted to make sure you were safe and to warn you to watch your back. I know he has friends with his same evil mentality and we're so close to getting you home that I don't want anything to happen to you."

"I'm good. I got my own eyes in here. I stay prayed up. How's my big cousin doing?"

She smiled at his bravery and faith. "Well. He's decided not to do anymore long hauls so he can be at home more, which is a good thing."

"But you feel like he's doing it because my getting a new trial is putting your life and your family in danger."

"I'm not afraid of Ronald, the Klan, White Nationalist, Aryan Brotherhood or anyone else, and you know that. I've been serving God since I was fourteen, and He has never failed me and I know He won't now. I told your stubborn cousin that, but I understand his concern as well. By no means is it your fault what Ronald is doing. He's upset that Khan won't accept his beliefs. Khan knocked him out cold and is pursuing a relationship with an African America woman, my daughter's sorority sister, Royale Chastain. Yes, the one whose mother was caught having an affair with her daughter's then boyfriend. I'm sure once Ronald finds out, it will really get under his collar."

He leaned back in his chair, shaking his head. "It truly is a small world because my cellmate, Magnus, has a son named Matan. I believe is the guy who the mother was having an affair with." They both marinated on that for a moment before Kalid continued. "However, that isn't my gravest concern right now."

Nina lifted a questionable eyebrow. "What is?" she queried, taken by the news that he was linked to Khan and Royale. She hadn't met Magnus yet and wondered what his thoughts were about the current ordeal, especially now that Royce was pregnant by his son, or at least it was a fifty percent chance that it was Matan's child.

"Khan. Did he tell you I reached out to him? It's time that he knew the truth, and I want him to hear it from me before the trial," Kalid told her, his piercing hazel eyes gazing worriedly into her fire-lit brown ones.

"No, but before he left to visit Royale, he came to talk to me. I knew there was more on his mind, but Kisha interrupted the conversation, so whatever else was on his mind was left unsaid. I agree with you, it's time the truth was known, and you're the only one who can tell it. If he seeks my advice, I will advise him to come see you and listen with an open heart."

"Thank you, Nina. Thank you for watching over him like you have. I know that Khloe is smiling down from heaven, thankful for your friendship and dedication to him."

"Khloe was family, Khan is family, and I've only done what any God-fearing person would do. I pray for him, Khloe, even Ronald's ol' hating self. Khan will always be safe with me. I better head out. I'll be back later in the week to do Bible study with you all, and I'd like to meet Magnus."

"Consider it done, and tell Keith he can come see me more often since he's no longer doing the long hauls. Now you be safe, and I love you."

"I love you too, and I'm going to tell Nehemiah and Kisha the truth, let them know who you really are."

"Let me tell Khan first. After I speak to him, then you can tell the kids."

"Okay," she agreed and then said one last goodbye before leaving.

*   *

Royce sat in the backseat of the SUV, anger pulsating through her marrow. Her mind drifted through the past as she remembered how Lance Kirkland had used her body, manipulated her mind and caused her the worse pain when he forced her to abort her baby. She never mourned that loss, the loss of her child, the loss of her innocence, the loss of the woman she was supposed to be. The day her unborn child died, so did she. In place of the lonely child who was raised to love God was a doppelganger. She looked just like Royce, but her mentality was different, her actions were different, her soul was different, and her walk with God was different. She had been faking that Christian walk for years now, and she was done. How could she love and trust a God who allowed her to be raped continuously and took her unborn baby? That was a God who didn't deserve her praises or fidelity.

Now, here she was, pregnant again, father unknown, and loathed by the world, judged cruelly and she was hurt, angry and full of malice. Somebody had to pay for her pain. She wasn't going down alone, which was why she tipped off the media about her being with child. They had pushed her. Her father, mother, Matan, Royale and Grayling, her Gray, had pushed her away. He spoke to her without filtering his true feelings and now they would feel her asperity. She was going to get on all the news channels, daytime talk shows and get her a mini-series to really embarrass her parents by letting the world know they allowed her to be subjected to sexual abuse. She was going to reach out to Strom and Magnus to show that nobody messed with Royce Chastain without getting burned.

They wanted to take her baby, yeah right, she would die a million deaths before she gave up another child. This baby she carried was going to love her like her family should have, and she didn't care who the father was. They had all turned their backs on her, and it was their faults that she was forced to seek retribution. She wanted to mend her relationships and seek forgiveness, but she didn't need that or them.

When she woke up this morning, she knew exactly what she had to do, and once she called Marc and they talked, it was all the confirmation she needed to move forward. Hell has no fury like a woman scorned, and she was scorned. She would take the greatest pleasure in getting each of them back, and for dessert, she would finally smite Roslyn. Her once ally and now her greatest enemy would be dealt with. Royce knew just how to get her. She was aware of why Magus was rotting in a West Virginian prison, but not everyone else.

At one time, Roslyn and Royce were friends and Roslyn introduced her to Grayling. As time progressed, Royce and Grayling grew closer. Eventually, Gray dumped Roslyn, but not before Royce, in her stupidity, confided in Roslyn about Lance raping her.

Apparently, Roslyn didn't deal with the rejection well and had been patiently plotting for a way to get back at Royce, but it ended up biting Roslyn in the butt. What happened was Roslyn had broken into Lance's house with the intention of robbing him and setting Royce up to take the fall. What ended up happening was the maid called the police and Magnus and Roslyn were caught red handed, but Magnus took the fall. He would have been out a long time ago, but while he was locked up, he murdered another inmate, which was why he was now in a maximum-security prison. She was going to drop that bomb too. She bet once the truth was out, she would no longer be viewed as a villain, but the victim she truly was.

"What are you contemplating?" Marc asked.

"The demise of every person who ever hurt me. I really tried the good girl act, but it just didn't work. I wasn't created to be good, but I'll have a good time taking them all down."

Marc gave her a concerned glance.

"Don't look at me like that, Marc. We're about to get paid. I'm going to milk this cash cow, and then I'm going to degrade them like they did me. It's time to reveal the real me." She grinned like the Joker.

"Remind me to never get on your bad side. I'm lowkey scared right now," Marc admitted.

"No need. As long as you stay loyal to me, I'll be loyal to you, but if you betray me..." She purposely didn't finish the thought. She needed her patsy and the way to keep him was to make him scared of what she was capable of.

*　*

Roslyn double checked herself in the mirror. She wore a modest length dress that kissed her petite but curvy frame. Her face was natural with just a light pink gloss and only BB cream, and eye shadow that matched her skin. She didn't want to come off too thirsty, even though she was in a Grayling drought she wanted him so badly. She wanted to downplay her feelings.

She pulled out of the driveway, humming to the soulful sound of Tamela Mann. When she finally arrived at Grayling's home, a smile spread across her round face. Grayling's truck was parked outside of the garage. Hopefully, that meant they would be alone and she could move her plan into action. She got out of her crimson Volvo S90 and grabbed her muffin container and Dooney & Bourke handbag, threw her shoulders back and pranced up to the door like she was walking down a runaway. She knocked on the door and waited patiently for it to open.

She felt like a million bucks, like nothing could ruin her mood. She was prepared to fight as dirty as necessary to get Grayling back, and Royce had made it so easy. When Grayling opened the door, she offered him a flirtatious smile. He seemed shocked by her appearance, but forever the gentleman, he welcomed her into his home and she quickly entered.

"I made you some muffins. They're apple cinnamon, I know how you enjoy them," she replied to the unasked question. She sauntered into the kitchen as if she was the woman of the house, and if everything went as planned, she would be the woman in charge.

"Thank you, Sister Roslyn, I appreciate the gesture. Are you here to talk about Matan? He was a bit disheveled and upset after meeting Royale's friend when he arrived late last night, then he stormed out of here. I was actually on my way to his apartment to check on him."

Now that had Roslyn curious. One, because Matan had said nothing to her about coming to visit Grayling or Royale. Two, because she thought Grayling despised Matan and wanted nothing to do with him, but here he was, seemingly concerned about her son. Then again, Grayling truly had a heart like David, and he loved the Lord. She respected and admired those qualities, but she needed the street Grayling to come out of hiding and put it on her. That's what she really wanted.

Hearing Grayling clear his throat, her impure thoughts halted and went back to Matan. She assumed he was in his feelings and upset with her because he wasn't taking her calls. Then the ungrateful little Gremlin had the audacity to inform his father about her, telling his father she was into some nefarious activities. Ol' snitch baby had her blood pressure high and she wanted to slap his laterigrade gait straight. Shaking the thought of Matan's disloyalty, she slowly turned to toward Grayling and spoke, "I was unaware that Matan sought to make amends, but I applaud his effort. I came over to check on you and Royale. I know after finding out about the baby, you might need a friend, and I'm here for you, Grayling. I mean, we both need each other during this trying time. We used to be friends before we were lovers and I'm here for you," Roslyn told him, batting her eyes flirtatiously as she slowly ambled toward him. He was like a magnet, and she was strongly attracted. It was by the grace of God she had been able to hold her mule because she had been in love with Grayling since forever.

"Well, I appreciate the offer, but I think your son needs you a lot more than me. I had a really intense prayer session with God and called on some prayer warriors, so I'm on the mend," he replied, taking as many steps back as she took forward.

"Gray," she hummed as she advanced toward him, not at all deterred. This was her moment and she was going to get her man. She needed him to understand that he was the only man she ever truly loved and everything she ever did was to make it back to him and claim his heart. "I still have feelings for you. I never stopped loving you, and after seeing how Royce betrayed your trust, disrespected her vows and neglected her wifely duties...well, you and Royale deserve better, and let's face it, I'm what's better. I know you miss me as I've missed you," Roslyn stated confidently, finally backing him in a corner. She lifted her small hand up, cupping his cheek, her eyes gazed into his. "I know when we were in high school, I couldn't compete with Royce. She had more money, better clothes, and she spoke with an elegance I fail to have. She was older, but she never loved you like me and she sure isn't loyal. I miss you, Gray."

Grayling inhaled a deep breath before removing her hand and exhaling, causing her to frown in confusion. "Roslyn, it's not going to happen. I'm a married man, and my vows mean everything to me, even if they don't to my wife or you. I made an oath before God and I won't break it just because you think I'm weak in the flesh and will fall for your words. We don't work, Rossi, and we never did. It had nothing to do with Royce. Let it go and take yourself home and see about your son," he lectured.

Roslyn jerked her hand out of his and she dropped her head to hide her shame and embarrassment over how easily he had dismissed and chastised her, even after Royce had disrespected him for her son. Everything in her wanted to slap his face to knock some sense into him, but instead, she schooled her face, lifted her head back up and relaxed the rage kindling inside. She did love him, and he had yet again rejected her like she wasn't good enough. He had the audacity to say they never worked, but she remembered it so differently.

"I see. I apologize, I thought…" She paused for a second to collect herself. For a moment, she nearly lost her voice but quickly regained her regal posture. "Well, I thought you cared, but it's obvious you still love your wife and you never loved me. Enjoy the muffins. I won't bother you again and neither will Matan. Consider me gone. I know when I've lost and I know when I'm not welcomed. I'll just move my membership to another church," she quietly whispered. He had never spoken to her like that before, but as much as she desired him, he didn't have any place in his heart for her. She thought she had him when she shared that Royce was pregnant, but he didn't want a good woman like her. It was time to move on.

She smoothed out the nonexistent wrinkles on her dress, only because she needed to do something with her now trembling hands. It angered her that he had such an impact on her, but she had none on him. She inhaled and exhaled, then turned to leave. As soon as her eyes left him, the tears flooded her face. Royce had won—again.

"Rossi, wait. You don't have to move your membership from the church, and I do care about you, but not in the way you need. It won't ever be like that for us, never."

"I got it, Bishop Chastain." She purposely addressed him that way to distance herself. "Believe it or not, even though I lack master and doctoral degrees, I know how to read between the lines. It's all good. I won't continue with the lawsuit, nor will I continue in my pursuit of you. If you want to stay married to a she-devil, then so be it. I wish you all the best, but I'm tired of sitting on the sidelines. You said what you meant and I've received it. Goodbye," she stuttered, unable to maintain her emotions. She made a lot of mistakes to get back to Grayling, one that caused Magus to be locked up, but Grayling didn't want her and there was nothing she could do but accept it, even though acceptance was breaking her heart.

* *

Royale sat Indian style on the back lawn of her house, smiling at Khan. She was happy to have him in Virginia. Since they were in the beginning stages of their relationship, she wanted to have him around all the time. His presence just felt right.

"What's up, Honey Drop? You said there was something you wanted to tell me."

That she did. Matan never knew about what happened during her childhood. She kept it hidden, but she wanted, no, she needed things to be different with Khan. He had shared with her his deepest agonizing pain and she wanted to do the same. She didn't want anything to taint what they were creating.

"Royale, what's the matter? Is it about the less than warm reception your family gave me? It's okay, you know once they get to know me, they'll be Khan crazy," he joked, showcasing his deep dimple.

"No, it isn't that. I have to tell you something about my past, and I don't know how you'll feel about it or me after, but I want you to know."

A confused scowl etched his perfectly carved face as he nodded, knowing that whatever was plaguing her mind was serious. So, he pulled her over and rested her on top of his lap. He rested his large index finger and thumb under her chin and she melted into him. "Nothing you can tell me will make me love you any less or leave you. Tell me what it is, we'll pray about it, and work it out."

She smiled at his words and was so thankful to God that He had brought Khan into her life. Taking a deep breath, she started to tell him about how she and Royce drifted and about Larry. The tears started to fall and she tried to hide away from Khan, but he wouldn't let her move. Instead, he drew her face closer to his lips and kissed each tear. "I love you, Royale, and what happened to you wasn't your fault, just like you told me what happened to my mother wasn't mine. The scripture says in Revelation 21:4, *He will wipe every tear from their eyes. There will be no more death' or mourning or crying or pain, for the old order of things has passed away.* It hurts now, but it won't hurt always, and whatever pain you are feeling, let me carry for you. You're beautiful and special and everything that has happened to you, all the pain, it has a purpose. You're strong, babe. I knew that the night I fixed your tire," he declared as he caressed her cheek.

"Believe me, I get it. You get worn, you have battle scars, but you also have God, and you have me. Neither of us will ever leave you, no matter what you do, what you face, what you fail at, God will be there and so will I. Don't cry, Honey Drop. I don't like to see you hurting like that."

She looked up at him, her eyes glistening with unshed tears. She reached her hands up and rested them on either side of his face and kissed him. "I love you, Khan. Though it hurt when I saw Royce and Matan together, I'm thankful, because if not for their deceit, I would have never met you."

He blushed. "I love you too. Can I pray for you?" he asked.

She smiled, recalling when she asked him the same thing when they went hiking in West Virginia. "Of course."

"Dear Heavenly Father, we come to You with humble hearts asking You to cleanse us of the pain of our past. Show us how to be good servants to You, for You and to one another. Heal all our wounds, God, and show Royale just how wonderfully and fearfully made she is. Teach her Father that she is worthy of Your love and that the sins committed against her are not a reflection of her, or punishment because whatever You take, You give back better than before. Only You can turn ashes into beauty.

"God, I love Royale. I thank You for allowing us to meet. I ask, Lord, that You allow me to be as much a blessing to her as she is to me. Before her, I didn't think I was worthy of Your love or hers. My father's constant hate and mistreatment made me believe I was nothing, but she has shown me that nothing and no one is beyond Your reach. She's gifted me with the knowledge that I am someone.

"God, I'm Your humble servant, scarred by blood, beaten down by the words of my earthly father, and I ask You to come into my heart. I want to be the man Royale deserves, and I want to be the son You created, so Father, forgive me my sins against You," his voice quivered, but he stayed steady, knowing that this was the Holy Spirit leading him because he felt so free and unburdened. Royale's grip on him tightened as love poured all over her at Khan's sincere words.

"Forgive my trespasses, and make me new. Mold me, Father, as a man worthy of Your daughter Royale. Teach me to be what she needs, build in me a heart of love like King David, wisdom like King Solomon and forgiveness and faith like Stephen the Martyr. Teach me Your ways so that when the time comes, I can be the kind of husband that leads with Godly insight. I love You, God, and I accept You in my heart. I love Royale, and I beseech You to heal her every physical and mental hurt and give my voice the words to make her feel protected and loved always. In Jesus' Name, Amen."

"Amen," Rina replied, crying.

"Rina?" Royale's head snapped up. She had fallen so deeply in sync with Khan's prayer that she had forgotten where she was. His honesty and vulnerability gave her chills.

Both girls had tears in their eyes. Royale's heart was fluttering at the sincere request that Khan had asked God on their behalf. She had fallen in love with him in that moment, and she was glad that Rina heard it as well. She needed Rina to know that Khan wasn't a monster, he was a broken man who needed to be mended by the love of God, and now he was. She'd prayed continuously for him to be healed, and now she needed to pray like that for Matan and Royce. She, too, wanted to be the woman Khan deserved.

"I'm sorry, I didn't mean to eavesdrop, I was looking for you and I stumbled upon you both here and heard Khan praying so poetically. I just prayed too. I..." She paused for a moment to wipe her tears. "My goodness, I pray that I find someone to pray for me like that. He gave me goosebumps.

"Khan, I apologize for judging you, and please forgive me for giving you the cold shoulder. You really love her, and it's a sincere love. That was a beautiful prayer. Thank you for loving her so much and praying for her. I'm overprotective of Royale, and that can make me blind, but I believe your love is truly blessed. Not that you need it, but you have my blessing," Rina finished, then turned and headed back into Ma Gwendolyn's house.

Royale wanted to call her back, but she sensed that Rina needed a moment. She turned her attention back to Khan. "Khan, you just got saved, like, you just accepted Christ in your life. Oh, baby, I'm so proud of you. That prayer to ask God on my behalf to heal my brokenness, baby, I love you. No one has ever prayed for me like that. I thought you were about to speak in tongues. I felt that in my soul. I felt the Holy Spirit in you. Khan, you are extraordinary. God is using you and your testimony is so powerful. You're mending me, Khan. You're taking my broken pieces and you are putting them back together. I'm thankful to God that He chose you for me," she rushed out, embracing him.

"We're going to make it, Khan. Our kind of love, this kind of love is forged in God and no man, no hate, no past can ever sever it. We're God strong, Khan," she whispered, as she unbound his hair, their foreheads touching. "I'm going to call you my Samson. You're so strong, and all this pretty hair. And no, I'm not Delilah, I'm your virtuous woman," she teased. "You know everyone is running around wanting to be Bonnie and Clyde, well, I aspire for us to be Boaz and Ruth."

"Me too, Honey Drop. If I knew it felt this freeing to be saved, I would have done it a long time ago. Once I get back to West Virginia, I want to get baptized. I want you to remember, no matter what, I'm not leaving you, I won't betray you, and I'd die a thousand deaths to protect you."

She rested her head on his chest, knowing he spoke nothing but the truth. "I would do the same for you. Let's celebrate, my baby is saved."

Chapter 7

Khan sat nervously at the restaurant owned by Patty Royce, a woman who he adored. She was just as sweet and warm as her granddaughter, and she could cook. After spending an entire day with the women, he felt as if they all liked him. Rina wasn't skittish of him anymore and welcomed him with open arms. Now he had to deal with the men in Royale's life and they just didn't seem as open as the women.

In fact, they hadn't been overly welcoming or polite to him, but they hadn't been rude either, although he got the feeling they didn't care for his arrival.

Khan, the General, Grayling, and Antwon were the only other people in the restaurant. It was a bit of a subdued mood. They hadn't come to eat, though there was a spread that had him salivating. No, these men in Royale's life came to interrogate him and he understood why when he briefly met Matan, but they needed to know he wasn't Matan.

The General's steel brown eyes burrowed into his, attempting to intimidate him, and if he were a lesser man, he would have. But Khan had witnessed his mother being murdered, been raised by a racist, retired police officer, who abused him at will and had just had his business nearly burned to the ground and had just recently become a saved man. No, he wasn't intimidated by these men of God. He respected that they loved Royale so much they were willing to go this far to ensure her safety. It was due to that respect and his love for Royale that he was going to tell them the truth before they asked. He wanted them to know he had nothing to hide and that his feelings for Royale were real.

"General, Bishop Grayling and Mr. Antwon, I'm sure you have done a background check on my family and myself, and if you haven't, then let me tell you who I am." He took a deep breath and began to tell them his story. "As a child, I witnessed my mother being murdered. I don't recall it well, I just remember shouts, cries, and blood, so much blood, but after that, my dad lost his mind. I'm not sure if he was always racist, or if it developed due to my mother's death. At any rate, he is a member of Christian Identity and the Klan. He hates, but I don't. I'm not friends with Royale as a fluke or to get back at my father." He paused, his long legs bouncing as he shared his story. He looked at each man, attempting to get a read on their thoughts, but they gave nothing away, so he continued. "All I know is that I was driving home and saw a woman in need and I helped her. We clicked.

"She's my gift from God. Her presence, her faith, her love for God has and is transforming me. I respect her, and her beliefs. She's helping me with my walk with Christ and helping me gain a closer relationship with God. You all have raised a wonderful, respectful and lovely woman. I love her. I'm not afraid to say that or feel it. I told her before she left West Virginia and I'm telling you that I have plans on courting her. She's refreshing, and kind and her heart is so beautiful. You have my oath that I'll always protect her. I understand how you feel, like, who is this stranger, what can he offer Royale. I offer her my heart, my soul, I offer her fidelity, respect, and safety. I offer her all that I am. You may think it is way too soon for me to feel that strongly, but never in the Bible have I read a timeframe for how long people need to know each other to love them.

"However, I'll wait for as long as she needs. I haven't nor would I ever rush her because she is worth waiting for. All I ask is that you all give me a chance, and judge me based on me, not by the ignorant philosophy of my racist father or the tragic death of my mother. I'm my own man, not swayed by the thoughts and opinions of another. I'm not perfect, nor will I ever be, but I'll always be a perfect gentleman to Royale." He took a moment to calm the beating of his heart. When he thought of Royale, she always caused the increased beating of his heart. He carried on.

"I was decaying inside before I met your daughter. She breathed life back into me and I would never do anything or let anyone else do anything to jeopardize that. So, whatever hoops you want me to jump through, I will. Whatever questions you need to ask, I will answer. I've nothing to hide. I assure you that my feelings for Royale are true. I came here because she needed me and I'll come to her anytime she needs me, no matter where she is. I'm going to stay here for as long as she needs my support. You have my word that I'll never break her heart or break my promises to her." He finished strong and looked each of them in their eyes, letting them know his words were true. He clasped and then unclasped his hands and waited like a man on trial for their judgment of him.

It was silent for a moment as the men soaked up his words. He wasn't sure what they were thinking, but he knew they knew he spoke the truth. It was raw and real and he was unashamed to share how he felt about Royale. No one could ever tell him that God hadn't made Royale especially for him.

"Well, I didn't expect you to preach a sermon," Antwon spoke first, large hands clasped together as he held Khan's gaze. "I admire you, young man, for speaking your truth so earnestly. That was a good speech, but words don't mean nothing, actions speak the truth."

Khan nodded his understanding, his eyes staring right into Antwon's. "Agreed. I promise you my actions match my words. I'm cutting ties with my father after I confront him for burning my business and threatening the Byses. Watch me, and you'll see that I am a man of honor who cares deeply for Royale."

"Are you saved?" Grayling asked.

"I'm not baptized, but I've given my life to Christ. I did it yesterday when Royale and I were talking. I prayed for her and the Spirit just took over."

"Well, Matan was saved, too, but he still violated the commandments," the General added. "Really, being saved these days don't mean a hill of beans. It's like Antwon said, actions speak the truth. Please believe, young buck, I will be watching."

Khan noticed Grayling rolled his eyes. "You're on probation, Khan. If you betray her trust, you deal with all three of us."

Khan smiled. "I would expect nothing less."

"Good, now we can eat," the General announced with authority. Khan was getting used to his bossiness. The man commanded a room with just his presence, and Khan could see how he made it as an Army General so young.

Just as Khan was preparing to pile on the food, his cell went off. He frowned when he saw that it was Nehemiah. "Excuse me, I need to take this." Khan got up and answered.

"Khan, man, Kisha was in a bad car accident. They rushed her to the hospital. I don't know if she's going to make it!"

"What? What happened?"

"I don't know, my momma called me. I'm heading to the hospital, can you tell Royale, and come when you can?"

They hung up and Khan turned to the men and explained that he needed to get back to West Virginia and the General offered his jet for him to use. He agreed and they left and headed back to Grayling's house. In route to the house, he phoned Royale and told her what had happened.

*   *

Everleigh patched up the little cut over her eye, a glint of satisfaction etched across her face. She'd had a run-in with Kisha Byse, who had the audacity to confront her for putting her little darkie friend in her place. Kisha had gotten all in her face, letting her know if she tried that again, she would have her to answer to. Well, Everleigh didn't take to kindly to the threat, so she called some backup. They had a little fun with *Ms. I'm Bad Byse* and ran her off the road where her car smashed into the tree. She ought to be glad they didn't run her off a cliff. Everleigh wasn't sure if they killed her or not, but if she died, well, so be it. Black people didn't deserve to breathe the same air as her, especially ones who didn't know their place.

"Everleigh, what's going on?" her mother, Irene, demanded.

Everleigh turned to see her mother, who had red hair just like her. They looked alike, except Everleigh had her father's green eyes and not her mother's pale brown ones. Her mother wasn't as tall as her, standing a modest five feet six inches, and was model thin, thinking that if she kept her body toned and thin, Everleigh's father would forget his black mistress.

Yes, her father, Strom Evans, had gone deep undercover. He was supposed to get close to the now U.S. Senator Eli Peterson, who had a deep disdain for white nationalists. He wanted to push more stringent laws for hate crimes and domestic terrorism by making it a crime for those who donate funds to aid organizations, which was an overreach of power. If you asked her, they should have assassinated him and been done.

Her dad would come home to them and then go back to his other family. Well, her mother had no idea he had impregnated the other woman. Apparently, she had a black sister out there, and if she knew where said girl was, she would run her off the road too. Anyway, it was what fueled her hate. Her parents hadn't been the same since it all happened, which was why she legally changed her surname to her mother's maiden name, Jacobs, and not her father's surname, Evans. He had betrayed the family in the worse way.

"I had an accident, mom. I'm fine. It's all good. Strom Jr. and Heather abetted me in dealing with the trash."

"Everleigh, I'm all about white pride, but I don't want you apart of the violence. You can be proud of your heritage without hurting or hating other people. I told you I was wrong to travel that path; it nearly cost me my family. I know you're hurt by your father's betrayal, but I don't want you associating with the Klan or any other racist groups. We're done with that. Shame on you for involving Strom Jr."

She rolled her eyes. Her momma used to be the biggest supporter, but now, she was Jell-O soft. It was disheartening and embarrassing. Her mother finally noticed that she wasn't going to reply, so she left. Everleigh let out a sigh of relief. She couldn't stand how weak her mother was. She would never forgive her father for his betrayal of making an abomination with a black woman, but what angered her more was that he really loved his other family. Even now, he wanted to reach out to his other daughter, whoever she was. It irked her soul. She was his only daughter; he had her and two sons.

"Everleigh, what have you done?" her father practically parroted her whining mother. Like his sleazy self had any right to interrogate her on her activities.

She rolled her eyes at the aggravating sound of her father's sharp tone. She just gazed at him through the mirror, challenging him with her refusal to speak. He was still a handsome man. He was six feet tall with a runner body build, dark chestnut hair and dark emerald eyes that always seemed to sparkle. They shared the same angular nose, round cheekbones, and moon chin.

He tipped his head up, signaling that he had enough of her attitude, so she answered him.

"I was accosted by a monkey and I did what any animal catcher would do: I dealt with it," she jeered, knowing it would get a rise out of him.

He let out a long breath, emerald eyes afire with anger and regret. "The racial epithet was unnecessary. We aren't those people anymore. I told you to stop that. We don't follow those teachings. I was wrong to ever insist that we did. I was wrong to make another family on your mother. I accept that, but you don't have to choose this path. Let that go. I'm here. I've been here, and we all know it's not black people you hate, it's me. So, get it out of your system and let's get through this. If I ever hear a slur like that leave your lips again, it's going to get ugly."

Her heart was pumping so fast, she could barely catch her breath. "It's been ugly. I do hate black people, the subhuman beast, and I hate the abomination you created with that other woman. I hate them all. They're a bunch of leeches who tore my family apart. Now, one is sticking her virus-laced talons into Khan. I should run her off the road and kill her too. I'm tired of losing to the *three-fifths.* Yes, I abhor you, too, now get out of my way," she screeched as she pushed him aside and bolted out of the house.

* *

Khan and Royale arrived at the hospital and quickly found the Byse family. They were sitting in a private room. From the information Khan could get, Kisha was currently in surgery. She had blunt force head trauma, internal bleeding, and they weren't sure if she would make a full recovery. The entire time on the private plane, Khan and Royale were praying. She had even called her father and asked him to pray as well.

"Ne, are there any updates?" Khan asked. Royale was right at his side, her arms wrapping around his waist, her pretty eyes glowing with unshed tears.

Nehemiah stood before him, a man apart. Khan was worried because Nehemiah didn't get upset or overly emotional. He was always calm, thoughtful, observant, slow to speak and quick to listen.

"What is it, Nehemiah?" Royale's candied voice queried.

"I don't want to alarm either of you, but this wasn't an accident. The police, due to a witness, believe it was road rage, but I overheard my mom tell my dad that she felt she was being followed. So, I believe with all my heart this is the beginning of Ronald's payback, and I told you, Khan, if your dad came for my family or Royale, I was coming for him," Nehemiah fumed with venom in his voice.

"I got your back, Ne, but are you sure? I mean, why go for Kisha and not me again? What has she ever done to anyone?"

"Neither of you are going to do anything. We don't know for sure what happened. Don't allow yourselves to become poisoned by bitterness and bound by iniquity. If you are right, Nehemiah, then we must combat hate with love and forgiveness, like Ephesians 4:25-32. Kisha wouldn't want you seeking revenge. Vengeance is mine says the Lord," she replied passionately.

Nehemiah turned his weary, dark tawny eyes toward Royale, his lips curled, his face wet with sweat either from worry or nervousness and replied, "Have you forgiven your mother or your ex-boyfriend for their trespass against you? Don't preach to me when my little sister is fighting for her life because she was born black. I know what I feel in my heart, and if Ronald didn't do it, then one of his cronies did. I'll hunt them down like the cowards they are to the end of Earth and in between," he snapped.

Khan pushed Royale behind him and got in Nehemiah's face. Nehemiah was his best friend, he loved him like a blood brother, but in no way was he going to allow him to come at Royale. "I understand you're upset, but don't take that tone with Royale. She loves Kisha, too, and doesn't want you to do anything irrational. I expect you to apologize to her because we're on the same team here. You have my word that if this has anything to do with my pops and his people, I will be right by your side. Right now, we need to be praying for Kisha and supporting your parents. Take a walk, cool down and let's think logically."

Nehemiah nodded in acquiescence. "You're right. I'm just so pissed off. I'm sorry, Royale."

"It's okay, but you're right as well. I can't ask of another, something I'm not practicing as well. I'm sorry too. I just don't want anything to happen to you or Khan, nor do I want either of you to do something you might regret."

Nehemiah nodded as he wiped his face off.

Khan turned to Royale and asked her to check on Mama Byse while he and Nehemiah went for a walk. She agreed and he watched her walk off before turning his attention back to his best friend. The pair walked to a nearby vending machine.

"Ne, for real, do you think Ronald did this?"

"All I know is that after Everleigh went ham on Royale, Kisha was livid. She said that if she saw Everleigh, she was going to confront her. A few days later, she's fighting for her life after being run off the road. After your dad set your company on fire and hung those scarecrows with our names on them, the threat is real. Then my mom said she's being followed. This has to do with your dad either directly or indirectly," he concluded.

He didn't want to believe it, but it did seem like something

Ronald and Hoss would do and that angered him. He needed to confront Ronald and cut off all ties with him for good. "Okay, let's get Kisha squared away and then I'll handle Ronald."

"Nah, we'll both handle Ronald."

When the pair returned, the doctor who performed the surgery was talking to Nehemiah's parents, so they rushed over, but by the time they did, all they heard was sorry.

"Sorry?" Nehemiah and Khan parroted.

That was when Khan saw Royale drop to her knees, tears streaming down her closed eyes while she prayed. He started shaking his head no, as he and Nehemiah rushed over to the family. Khan rested a hand on Royale's back. Her entire body was trembling, causing his heart to break, but he had to hear the words.

"She's gone, Nehemiah. Her heart wasn't strong enough to survive the surgery. My baby girl is dead...she's dead," Nina loudly whispered before collapsing into her husband, who mirrored her devastation.

Nehemiah looked at Khan. Words weren't spoken, but the understanding was loud and clear.

* *

Ronald hung up the phone with Everleigh and grinned. She was definitely the right kind of woman for Khan. She took initiative, and he was proud. That darkie, Nina's daughter, insulted and threatened Everleigh like she had the right, and Everleigh showed her when she ran her off the road. It just made his day. That Byse family would learn to stay in their place sooner or later. He was basically on cloud nine until Hoss interrupted his celebratory fest followed by Wiley. Wiley wasn't officially Klan, but he hung around and was on the police force. He was a member of the Christian Identity and a good friend, who he trusted on missions like these.

"Hoss? Wiley?" he asked as his friends sauntered into the office without a knock. That meant something was up.

Hoss sighed, making his rotund belly jiggle a little. His rosacea-stained face seemed redder if that were possible. He looked like a glowing stop sign, which caused Ronald concern. Wiley didn't look much better.

"Ron, it's worse than we thought. Your boy is messing with a muddy and it's one of them educated, high and mighty types. The ones who got their talons in Strom and nearly broke up his family. I swear them coloreds got devil magic."

"What?"

"It's Eli Peterson's freaking granddaughter. The same rats that were on that reality show about first ladies. I had the boys do a little digging. You remember that trollop that was all on television for being caught having an affair with her daughter's boyfriend?"

Ronald nodded, hoping this wasn't leading to where he thought it was.

"Well, he's with the daughter. It's bad, but then it's good because we can wipe out Eli Peterson now. Well, the Virginia chapter of the Brotherhood can. They want him too."

"He's dating a colored?"

"Yep, got her all in his mouth like she's the yellow pack of Lay's potato chips. You know what they say 'bout them chips, you can't eat just one. She done worked her voodoo on him, just like they did Strom. We can't have this again," Hoss quipped and opened the folder to show him the evidence.

Ronald was so livid; he threw his beer and the effort shot pain throughout his body. The pain reminded him that he needed to see a doctor, though he was sure his medical issue stemmed from his son acting like a jerk.

Khan was going to make Ronald kill him. His son had gone to Virginia to visit a colored, and by the photos, it seemed Hoss was correct in saying they were dating. It enraged him on a level that he couldn't adequately articulate, but Khan was going to get a lot of people killed. Not only had he managed to lose a good woman like Everleigh, but he had chosen a darkie who was the granddaughter of an enemy of the Klan and other white supremacists, Eli Peterson. He was all about equal rights, and harsher punishments for hate crimes and extending the laws. He'd been doing that since he was first elected, which was why Strom had been used to take him out, which he failed to do, but it wasn't his fault, black women were touched by the devil. It looked like his son was about to get the same Satan's kiss.

"Well?" Hoss and Wiley both asked simultaneously.

"It's time to turn up the heat. We need to contact the boys in Virginia and let them reign terror. I want to know everything about Eli Peterson's family and this girl. I mean everything. It's time to properly introduce them to the New Era!" he hissed.

Chapter 8

Silence. Mo flowing tears or whimpers, no hiccups, sniffling or God why conversations, just quiet that seemed to have no end. Numbness came next. A numb misery had overtaken everyone, all too in shock to truly comprehend the four-letter word—dead. It was a defensive measure, a refusal to feel, to believe that Kisha Byse was indeed dead. If Nehemiah's hypothesis was correct, it was no accident, but a deliberate attempt on her life in a revenge attack all orchestrated by Khan's father or his supremacist group.

Was it simply the musing of a brother's broken heart, or was it the truth?

The distant sounds of Tamela Mann's "I Can Only Imagine" played on the radio. Usually, the melodious hum of her voice soothed Royale, but tonight, it was only a reminder that her dear friend had departed to the other side. Sadly, Royale couldn't remove the weeping of Nina, the distress of Keith or the agonizing grief of Nehemiah. She was drowning in their sorrow, and she was fighting giving into her anxiety.

Taking deep breaths to calm the anxiousness, she tried to compartmentalize the pain, only to open another door. Flashes entered her mind: her friend's eyes closed, body lukewarm dressed in bruises, mouth slightly agape, hands flat atop white sheets. She looked as though she was sleeping, just waiting for a prince to kiss her lips to wake her, but Kisha wasn't ever coming back, at least not to this place. That was a truth too hard to accept and too difficult to comprehend. The emotions she felt now

—rage, revenge, sorrow, fear—created a combustible concoction that if allowed to fester and be released, would surely stain her soul. *Let it go, pray, believe in God.* She heard the inner whisper but was unable to listen.

Royale's toned, thick form was balled up like an infant in Khan's warm embrace. His warmth was her survival. His warmth was her sanity, her last defense to not give into the cold, cruel brutality of revenge.

Khan hadn't spoken a word since he attempted to stop Nehemiah from running off. Instead, Khan had dropped to his knees and wept like a child. She held him, believing that he was more than likely recalling the night his mother was murdered and those old feelings of guilt, remorse, love and loss replayed in his mind. His calming blue eyes were now grief-stricken orbs of a dull, depressed blue, a color she had never witnessed before. Maybe it was because while in his embrace, she stole his strength, his energy, his calmness. She needed it all just to breathe, but he needed it too. He had taken a physical blow. He was stuck between a family who loved him and a father who only loved him with stipulations. Though the investigators hadn't pinpointed a suspect, Nehemiah had. It was draining Khan.

"Honey Drop?" Khan's drawled cadence called out. His voice was soft and mellow but still startled her as she was ruminating, reliving the horrid moment of death. She looked up and noticed they had arrived at the Byse family home. She didn't even recall the drive. She eased off his lap with his assistance, her tender, tear-laced honey copper eyes dancing around the perimeter, accessing its safety, unsure if Khan's father wanted to seek more revenge.

Slowly and under the protection of Khan, who had one arm to secure her, the other holding their travel bags, they followed behind Nina and Keith. It was late now, the sun back in its hiding place and the somber moon hanging in the sky. Something about the night just seemed unsettling.

Her tired eyes watched as Keith unlocked the door, telling

Khan to stay with her and Nina as he checked the house. It seemed that Nehemiah's belief had become his father's. No one felt safe anymore.

After checking, he told them to come in, and due to being exhausted beyond belief, Royale slowly ambled up the stairs and headed right into the shower. There she allowed herself to let it all out. She cried for everything and everyone. For losing Kisha, for losing Royce, for losing Matan, for losing her innocence when Larry touched her all those times, and for the physical abuse she witnessed Gwendolyn suffer at the hands of Strom. She cried for Khan and the Byse family. As she wept, the pain seeped through her pores, burning like acid, but no longer poisoning her body. It was cleansing.

She wanted to be free. She needed to be the best woman to Khan, the best daughter, the best friend and until she heard the words of her friend being dead. She hadn't known how much bad energy and toxic thoughts she held. It was time to let it go, grieve her friend, and fight evil with good. Could she? Was she that strong in her faith that she could hand it over to God and love her enemies, and pray for those who prosecuted her like Matthew 5:44 clearly required? Could she do as God asked in 1 John 4? Could she love those who seemed unlovable?

"I don't know, God. I just know that I'm soul sick and I need relief. Help me, God. Help the Byse family, Khan and me to overcome this hate with love. My friend is gone all because of what? Skin tone? Because she had a fearless heart and called out injustice? Because she and her family love Khan like a family should? Is that my fate? Will I be killed because I love Khan? I do my best to never question you, God, but why? Why take her? No parent wants to bury their child. Forgive me, Father, I have no right to question You, I just need Your guidance. Help, God, please help," she lamented in a soft whisper before turning off the shower, getting out, drying off her wrinkled skin and getting dressed.

Once she was done, she collapsed on the bed, the same bedroom she had when she stayed less than a week ago when Kisha let her cry on her shoulder. Would she be alive if Royale had never come? Feeling herself going into that dark place, she picked up her phone to distract her mind. She was about to click on the Bible app when she noticed she had two messages, one from her father and the other from Rina. She had called them both to let them know what had happened. The screaming of Rina nearly stole her resolve. Royale was the strong one, yet tonight, all she felt was weak, like her bones were brittle and every breath was like trying to climb Mt. Everest without an oxygen mask.

Unlike when her mother and Matan betrayed her, she couldn't run. Instead, she had to take each lash from the invisible whip, and it was depleting her. She heard that whisper again. Philippians 4:6-7, *Do not be anxious about anything, but in everything… And the peace of God, which transcends all understanding, will guard your hearts and your minds in Christ Jesus.*

"Honey Drop." His voice sounded so distant, yet was so near. It pulled her out of her reverie.

Royale snapped her head up, glancing at Khan. Her gentle giant had morphed. His chiseled face that was always model perfect showcased his weariness. His eyes glowed with a sea of hurt, cheeks sunken, and those thumb perfect dimples hidden. His hair rested wet and unbound, scattered messily atop his head. His broad, Viking-like shoulders were slumped like he was carrying a cross far too heavy to bear, as he slowly shuffled almost at a turtle's pace. His vibrant, tanned skin burned a furious crimson, painted with sorrow and agony. She felt her heartbeat decreasing. All that energy, strength and calmness she stole from him, he needed back. With a trembling chin, eyes laced with guilt from stealing from him, she widened her arms, welcoming his tattered body, his bruised soul a home in her embrace. "Come here, Khan. I'm so sorry, my love."

He moved in her direction with the speed and grace of a gazelle. He was hungering for whatever comfort and affection she could offer. It was her turn to allow him to ball up like an infant and just be consoled and loved on, and she was more than willing to do that. She owed him safety, reassurance, and love. The weakness that had overtaken her before was slowly fading.

Thank God, it was a king size bed. Khan stretched his large body at an angle and rested his head on her lap. She ran her finger through his damp hair and began to sing the lullaby that her grandmother Patty used to sing "All Through the Night", which was a hauntingly beautiful Welsh song. As Royale sung, her fingers tenderly caressed Khan's face but stopped when she felt the tears soak up her granny gown.

"How did you know?" his weakened voice questioned.

It was then she noticed his body was shuddering. "Know what?"

"That my mom used to sing that to me. My family is of Welsh descent and that was one of her favorite lullabies she sang to calm me until I was about five."

"My grandmother sang it to me as well, and for some reason, God put it on my heart to sing to you." There was a long pause, and finally, Royale began to speak again. "I have a confession, Khan, one that I've realized while lamenting the loss of Kisha. I've been a bad representation of a Christian to you, but that ends tonight."

His long-toned body stiffened under her as she confessed to him. He turned slightly, gazing into her eyes, the dull, depressed blue gone, replaced with a calming blue topaz, the vibrant color she loved to see. He lifted his large hand, cupping her face. "What are you talking about?"

"When you came to my house, I had already snapped at Royce and was about to do the same to Matan. Nehemiah was right, I can't preach to him the Word if I refuse to live it too. Losing Kisha today just reiterated that. I need to repent. I need God's forgiveness for my actions and I'm apologizing to you. I need to set a better example, especially with you being a babe in Christ. Will you forgive me?"

"Yes, of course, but you didn't do anything wrong. You were hurt, your trust violated and it happens. You can only be like Christ, you can never be Him, and God knows that. He knows your heart, babe. You have a pure and genuine heart."

She nodded, and a weak smile covered her face. "You're good to me, Khan."

"You don't know how you've saved me, but I fear I may lose you too." She was about to speak to him to reassure him that she wasn't going anywhere, but he lifted his index finger to her lips to hush her reply. He sighed, and then sat up in the bed, the two of them face to face, eye to eye. "It's my fault. It all is, from Everleigh attacking you verbally to my dad threatening the Byse family to Kisha dying. That's two deaths on my hands, Royale, two. How can you ask me for forgiveness when my hands are dripping with blood?"

She shook her head and took each of his hands into her own and kissed them. "These are hands that have survived pain, death, and betrayal. These are hands that soothe me when I feel anxious, these are the hands that hold me and make me feel safe, these are the hands of love, protection, and God's beauty. These are the hands that prayed for me, the hands that accepted God, and these are hands that are renewed. Don't blame yourself for something that isn't your fault. I hurt, you hurt, but the Byse family has to bury a daughter, a sister and they need our strength, love, and assistance," she explained, feeling her resolve and faith in God renewed. She placed Khan's hands over her heart. "I love you, Khan, and I won't leave you no matter what comes next, you will have me until my body is no longer in this world.

"It's not my fault?" he queried childlike.

She leaned in and peppered him with kisses. "No, baby, it's not yours or mine. You're doing yourself an injustice by self-blaming. It's times like these we must draw nearer to God."

*　*

Nehemiah wanted to kill, but he didn't. It was like an invisible wall was present that wouldn't allow him to move. He did what any man of God would do, he prayed. Back in his college days, he had a buddy who was Catholic, and he had attended services with him, and one of the prayers he loved was *The Prayer of St. Francis of Assisi.*

Lord, make me an instrument of Your peace. Where there is hatred, let me sow love; where there is injury, pardon; where there is doubt, faith; where there is despair, hope; where there is darkness, light; where there is sadness, joy.

O, Divine Master, grant that I may not so much seek to be consoled as to console; to be understood as to understand; to be loved as to love; For it is in giving that we receive; it is in pardoning that we are pardoned; it is in dying that we are born again to eternal life.

He cried as each word was spoken. He knew that if he continued down this path of ill regard, malice and revenge, he would end up in prison or even dead, and then his parents would be childless. He believed in God and believed that God would set all that is wrong right, he just had to bow out and let love prevail, not hate.

Chapter 9

B ishop Grayling hopped on the private jet, he and the General were headed to West Virginia to check on Royale and offer their condolences to the Byse family. Grayling had also reached out to Timothy Hoover, who was a seasoned investigator from Georgia and a good friend because Tim's daughter, Olivia, had become good friends with Royale and Rina. They were working on linking their nonprofits to create an umbrella organization. Also, Tim Hoover's in-laws attended Grayling's church. Anyway, Grayling and the General knew all about Strom's association with Khan's father after doing an extensive background check. It was worse than they first thought, and the General, after finding out how Kisha died, and the information they got from Royale, didn't believe it was an accident either. It felt like a warning, and if that were so, then Grayling needed Royale back home where he could keep her safe ASAP. These were trying times and he wouldn't lose his daughter because these people chose to hate and not to love.

"General, are you sure it's safe for you to be here?"

"I wasn't intimidated during the Civil Rights Movement, and I darn sure won't back down because some cowards wearing hoods with hate pumping through their veins don't like the policies or legislation I create. The question isn't, is it safe for me, the question is, is it safe for them," he replied as he picked his book back up and carried on as if that statement explained everything.

* *

Strom let out a sigh. His long legs were crossed as he sat in his mahogany frame, burgundy vinyl chair. The ticking of his jawline was the only indication that he was mindful of his surroundings. He dropped his head, shaking it in shame and disbelief. His daughter was the one behind the road rage attack that had killed Kisha Byse. It was all over the news, and he would have never suspected his daughter until his son, Strom Jr., confessed everything.

Apparently, there was a lot more to the situation. Everleigh was jealous because Khan had moved on from her and to another woman, a black woman, but her identity was unknown to him, though he could contact Hoss or Ronald to get that information. It seemed that Kisha was defending her friend and that got under his spoiled daughter's skin. Instead of pulling hair and arguing, she called her brother and Heather to assist her in running a young woman off the road and killing her. Death wasn't the intention, but it was the result.

The police were looking for leads. They had a witness, so he assumed it was only a matter of time before the police came knocking at his door. Here he was, contemplating if he should turn her in for the crime she committed or protect her. He could always shoot for involuntary manslaughter, but he was sure he couldn't sweep this one under the rug. He was torn. He had made so many mistakes all in the name of power and control only to have broken the heart of both his wives and his children. Maybe this was him reaping what he sowed.

Letting out a sigh, Strom reached for his telephone and called his contacts. He wanted to know if this was an isolated incident or if his daughter was part of a larger revenge plot, and if so, he couldn't sit idly by and do nothing.

Chapter 10

Royale, Rina, and Livvy were all in the kitchen, cleaning up since the repast had ended. Khan, Canton, and Nehemiah were out back, sitting around the fire pit, just staring off into space. Sometimes holding a conversation among themselves, other times in deep thought. Nina and Keith Byse were in the family room with Bishop Grayling, who was counseling the family.

"That was a beautiful ceremony, and Royale, you and Nehemiah performing 'See You Again'. That was Kisha's jam, though. She had a serious crush on Paul Walker."

Royale giggled. "She sure did. Nehemiah suggested we do it, and Mr. and Mrs. Byse gave their consent," she replied, and the humor quickly turned into sadness. "I miss her. I keep thinking she'll come through the door, teasing me about Khan or fussing about something. Kisha was a real friend, as loyal as they come and her heart was on fire for Christ. She taught me to be fierce. If I had never met her my freshmen year of college, I don't know where I'd be."

"Kisha was one in a million. She taught me the importance of loving me and seeing myself in the same loving light that God does. She just had this ability to make the toughest situation easy," Rina added, her green eyes glowing in remembrance.

"I agree. She met my sister Tori first because you all know I was anti-sorority—it reminded me too much of my past life— but Kisha was just warm and inviting. That laugh, her laughter was contagious. I bet she's in heaven and has the angels flapping their wings they are laughing so hard," Livvy replied, wiping a tear from her gray eyes.

Royale moved in between Rina and Livvy and embraced them both. "Kisha lives on in all of us, each of us has a part of her. It'll hurt for forever, but the intensity of the pain will ease because we know that one day, there will be a great reunion. The Bible tells us in John 14:1-4, *Let not your hearts be troubled. Believe in God; believe also in me. In my Father's house are many rooms. If it were not so, would I have told you that I go to prepare a place for you? And if I go and prepare a place for you, I will come again and will take you to myself, that where I am you may be also. And you know the way to where I am going.* We must believe, pray and never cease praying until that empty hole we feel in our hearts is remodeled and filled with God. Remember, we all promised to be strong for the family. They need us and we them," Royale preached.

"Are you sure God isn't calling you to the pulpit?" Rina teased.

"I'm not sure, but wherever God leads me, I will follow."

Later that night

It was dark now, only the sounds of insects serenading and frogs croaking interrupted the serene night. Countless stars lit up the velvet sky, sprinkling about and showcasing God's brilliance and omnipresence. Tossed over Royale's brown, sun-kissed legs was an Afghan with her sorority's Greek lettering on it and snuggled behind her was a deep-sleeping Khan. The day had been long and emotional for him.

His Rapunzel length, golden hair rested on his body like a blanket. The harsh lines that had painted his face were gone. In sleep, he looked innocent, free, and peaceful. Ever since the death of Kisha, he had been more protective and refused to let Royale out of his sight, even in the Byse family home. She smiled at how deeply connected they had become and how she, too, would die to save him. It sounded so Shakespearean, and yet it was true. Death had brought them closer.

Shaking the thought, she placed her bookmark into the book

she was reading; it was Olivia "Livvy" Hoover's memoir, *The Devastation and Deliverance of Dinah*. It was indeed a powerful, thought-provoking read, and Royale understood why so many people were touched after reading it and why it was an instant bestseller. She closed the book and placed it down on the round, hand carved table and then closed her eyes. She had no intentions of sleeping, no, she was thinking. Thinking about how she didn't want to be angry or vengeful. Thinking that God created her not to judge but to forgive, and she hadn't offered that forgiveness to Royce, Matan, or even Strom. She had allowed her emotions to overcome, and instead of praying to God for healing and love, she chose to lean on her own understanding. Losing Kisha just opened her eyes to what she was missing because no matter what her mother did, or Matan, they were still God's children. The same God who died and overcame death for her sins had done the same for them. It was her Christian duty to forgive. That didn't mean they had to be best friends, but it meant respect, it meant to love, it meant to heal. She had to let it all go because as she told her friends, she wanted to be part of the great reunion of all those souls gone before and she didn't want to be left behind.

"Royale, Royale!"

The voice sounded familiar. It sounded like home, but it was distant. Had she drifted off to sleep? The soft tug of her exposed arm confirmed her unconscious thought. She had dozed off while thinking. She slowly opened her eyes to find her father bent over, his calming, dark eyes gazing worriedly into hers. "Daddy, I'm fine. Khan and I just settled out here to talk, but he went to sleep as soon as his head hit my hip and I decided to catch up on some reading," she explained.

"I can see that. I came out here because it's been an extremely long day, but I needed to talk to you. Your grandfather and I must return to Virginia tomorrow. Before I leave, we need to discuss a lot."

Her face twisted in concern, not sure what her father had to say, but she nodded her acquiescence and lightly tapped Khan as she altered her body from a semi-supine position to sitting up-right. Seeing that Khan wasn't ready to wake, and knowing just how tired he really was, she shifted his head to her lap and then spread her Afghan over his body before turning her full attention to her father. When she looked over at him, he was smiling.

"What?"

"I can just really tell you care about him. The General and I were concocting a plan to end your little tryst, but it seems that the two of you aren't just a fling. I guess I knew that when the General had him sign a binding contract," Grayling chuckled.

Royale shook her head because she knew just how far her grandfather could go. "I can't even say I'm shocked, but I'm guessing that isn't why you sought me out. That little vein is about to pop out in your forehead, so what's the matter?"

He smiled. "You're just as astute in your observations as I am." He sighed as he reached for the deck chair and pulled it closer to his daughter.

Royale knew then, by the change in his facial features, that what he had to tell her was serious, but instead of going into full-on panic mode and running the risk of triggering an anxiety attack, she calmed her breathing and thought of Bible verses. Her father reached out and placed his smooth molasses-colored hand atop hers and squeezed.

"I'm going to tell you some things you didn't know, and the General is actually having this same conversation with Rina. We didn't keep this information from you, we only put it all together recently. It seems that these paramilitary hate groups have elephant memories and devil hearts." She gave her father a questionable look, but he continued. "See, when Strom met Gwendolyn, we had no idea until recently it was his way of getting into the family to get to the General. Your grandfather was adamant about hate crimes, civil rights, and creating a better America for you than he was subjected to during his younger years. In fighting, he became an enemy to a lot of people, mostly right-wing extremist. Strom was tasked with getting close to the family and finding the General's weakness. Why he married

Gwen knowing he was already married, I don't know, but I know he failed at his assignment. I also know that Strom and Ronald are linked; at least I know they know each other. Strom's daughter, Everleigh Jacobs—"

Royale gasped. "Daddy, I know her." Everleigh Jacobs was Strom's other family, meaning she was Rina's sister, the same hateful spirited demon who verbally attacked her and the one who still wanted Khan. That was a revelation she was unprepared to deal with. She thought she had heard the last of Everleigh Jacobs, but apparently, she was wrong.

"How?" Grayling queried, sounding astonished.

"She…she was, oh my gosh." Royale's voice trembled. "I didn't tell you this, but she verbally assaulted me. Told me she wasn't afraid of me and that the next time we met; she'd have a slave kit. I can't believe that woman is Rina's sister," she replied despairingly.

"I don't understand, when did you cross paths with her? As far as I know, Strom doesn't live here in Charleston. I thought he resided two hours away in Morgantown."

"I don't know. I haven't seen or heard from him, but I have met his daughter," she replied as she attempted to rouse Khan. She knew he needed his sleep, but he also needed to hear this newfound information. After another shake, his tired eyes ripped open, and he gave her a startled look. She instantly felt sorry for waking him up. "I'm sorry for waking you up, Khan, but my dad has just shared some intel I think you need to hear, and maybe you can assist him as well."

It seemed her voice drew him out of his zombie-like trance and he sat up and looked right at her father. Grayling proceeded to share with him what he told Royale.

"Do you think she knows who Royale is, that she's the General's granddaughter? If she does, then so does my father." Then he looked over at Royale. "Honey Drop, you need to leave with your family. I don't think being here is safe for you. If they were willing to send in Everleigh's father to marry into your family, I'm sure they are desperate enough to cause you harm as well. I can't allow that," he replied earnestly.

"We don't know what they're planning. They've had time to come after me. I've been in the limelight with Royce forever, and nothing. I won't run based on conjecture and fear. I serve a God far stronger than mere men. I'm not running anymore, ever, from anything," Royale stated stubbornly with her arms crossed in defiance and her honey copper eyes, which were more copper now, dared her father or Khan to disagree.

"Well, if you stay, you can't go off alone," Khan dictated and Grayling chuckled.

"Listen, honey, I don't want you making rash decisions. Please pray about it and what God puts on your heart, I will accept. Khan is right, you need to be cautious whether you come home with me or stay with the Byse family. While you two were out here, the police came by, and they are indeed investigating this as a homicide. Someone intentionally ran Kisha off the road. I don't know if their intent was murder, but that was the result."

Royale blinked back tears. In her heart of hearts, she knew it was no accident. However, hearing that the police agreed was like detaching her heart from her body. All she could imagine was the fear Kisha must have felt. Before a tear could fall, Khan swallowed her into his arms, allowing her head to rest upon his chest. "We'll get justice for Kisha, and I'll make sure no harm comes to you. If Everleigh is involved, nothing on this Earth will protect her," Khan vowed.

Chapter 11

G rayling, Rina and the General were back in Virginia, each lost in their own thoughts with Grayling thinking just how small the world was. For some reason, they just couldn't rid themselves of Strom and his band of misfits. They were like ants. You destroy one mound only for them to escape and create another one bigger.

As soon as he entered his home, the phone rang. He answered, "Hello?"

"Bishop Grayling, it's me, Marc. I know I'm the last person you want to hear from, but I had to reach out to you because your wife is really on the edge. As of late, all she is spouting off about is revenge and bringing everyone down with her and getting a new reality show. I don't know what she knows or how true her threat is, but she's no longer attending any counseling sessions. It's like she's done a complete one-eighty. Maybe you, the General and Ms. Patty can stage an intervention because I'm concerned."

"Marc, I want to believe you, but this all smells like a setup. All you've been wanting is another reality show. If I were a betting man, I'd bet this staged intervention is going to be taped and that Royce wants it that way so she can excuse her horrid behavior and play the victim when she is the leading villain in a mess she created. Unless it deals with the baby, I would appreciate if you not call me, but feel free to contact Patty and the General," he replied calmly and hung up.

* *

Eli "General" Peterson entered his office with a thick envelope.

He unsealed it and pulled out the manila folder that held everything he needed to know about Ronald Masterson and his associates. Ronald had been a rotten apple since the death of his father, Jackson Andrew Masterson, who was a proud, card-carrying member of the Klan. He passed his hate to his son like it was an heirloom and that son tried to pass it on to his son. He was still astounded that his granddaughter was dating Ronald's son. They were all linked to Strom. He let out a determined sigh.

According to the file, Ronald was being investigated by Internal Affairs because he murdered an unarmed black man; it wasn't his medical condition that forced him to retire, though that was interesting as well. Old Ronald had more than just OA, his drinking had given him a heart condition and possibly a bad liver. More than likely death was creeping upon him, which would suggest his desperation for ending Khan's attachment to Royale. Ronald was coward enough to try.

Ronald was mistaken if he thought the General was going to lie down and not fight. When it came to his family, there was nothing he wouldn't do, which was why he only let Larry go after he had a long, private conversation with him. At any rate, Ronald Masterson, Everleigh Jacobs, and Hoss Cleveland were all on his list. With the help of the FBI, he was going to find out who caused Kisha Byse to run off the road, and ultimately, her death. If Ronald and his group had anything to do with it, he would do everything in his power to make sure those guilty never saw the light of day and stayed caged up.

Chapter 12

It was finally happening, yet Kalid couldn't be happy. One week ago, Kisha had died and was buried. He was still mourning the loss of Kisha Byse and he couldn't help but blame himself. Had he walked away from his beloved Khloe, she would be alive now, and Ronald Masterson wouldn't be on a vindictive scheme to take down his family. He sighed as he made his way to visit Khan. It was time for the truth to be revealed. He was nervous and scared. He had no idea how Khan would react, especially with him grieving Kisha, who was like a sister to him.

"You got this, Kalid," Magnus told him.

Kalid nodded and was escorted by his guards to the visiting section of the prison. As he walked, shackled, with prison-issued clothing, all he thought about was how to start off the conversation with Khan. Before he realized it, there he was. He knew it was Khan because of the description Nina had given him. He was a tall young man, built strong like his uncle, but there was still that little boy in him. He didn't offer Kalid a smile, which he understood. To him, Kalid was a stranger, a man who he was told all his life murdered his mother, but that was a lie, all lies. He would and could never hurt Khloe. He loved her. He would always love her.

"Hello, Khan," Kalid finally spoke, though his voice sounded foreign, even to him. It was unsure and a little shaky. He hoped Khan wouldn't misjudge him for that. Seeing Khan was like looking at Khloe. He had some of her features, the cheek, chin and those deep dimples.

"Well, you said you wanted to tell me the truth and I came to hear your side of the story. I'm doing this for Mama Byse. We just buried Kisha, my heart is heavy, but because I love Mama Byse and she insisted, I came. Even though I feel like my heart has been ripped out of my chest, I'm here. So, please don't lie to me, don't waste my time, and don't sugarcoat the truth. I would appreciate if you just give it to me real and uncut."

Kalid nodded in respect and did as he requested. He was impressed by the young man sitting before him. "First off, I'm Keith's cousin. The reason Nehemiah and Kisha didn't know about me was because the Byse family eschewed me. My mother is white, and my father was black; he passed away some time ago while I was locked up in here. He was also married. I'm the bastard Byse, though I carry my mother's surname.

"Keith didn't care about any of that. He welcomed me in as his cousin and he and Nina, were extremely close. I met your mother before she met Ronald. She was all sweetness and goodness, bright-eyed and beautiful, attending West Virginia University. She and I met at a party. We were instant lovers; she was so easy to love." He paused for a moment, recalling the beautiful memory. Then Khan cleared his throat, bringing him back to the present.

"So, I ended up joining the Marines so I could pay for college. I wanted to marry her before I left, but she told me she wanted to graduate college first and I respected that. However, she agreed to get engaged to me. I left, got shipped off, we had a huge argument, but I still loved her and wrote her, and she did the same, and then the letters got fewer in between. I got to leave and came to see her, and it was then I found out she was pregnant. Somehow, her little friends had gotten into her head that I was unfaithful and she believed them and moved on. I forgave her instantly. I knew it wasn't my child, but I didn't care. I told her I would marry her and raise the baby as my own, but she wouldn't hear of it. She was so ashamed of being unfaithful to me and I told her she was forgiven, but she wouldn't hear it.

"Broken as I was, I returned to camp, but not before reaching out to Nina and asking her to look after Khloe and her unborn child. A few years went by, and in that time, you were born; the first child she had died of SIDS. I finished up my time in the military. After you were born, I think she started to see your father in a different light. All I know is that she wanted us to start over and I was ready to do that. We were planning to run away with you and the child she was carrying. She was having my baby. She'd sent your father the divorce papers as soon as she found out she was pregnant. He was already deep into some racist philosophy, but when he found out about me, he lost it. It was your father who caused your mother's murder that night, Khan.

"He and his goons followed us, unbeknownst to me. I don't know if you recall that your mother and I had a cabin we were staying in, and you were with us, playing with your Hot Wheels and those little green soldiers. They rushed in and bound me. They were supposed to kill me and beat your mother, but that changed when your father discovered your mother was birthing my child, a child who would wasn't white.

"He was livid, and it was his hands that murdered your mother, not mine. He didn't know you were there because you hid when the commotion started. They set me up for the murder and left you there, so when you came to the room, you saw me holding your mother, sobbing as I watched the life leave her and our unborn child. I think the only other person who understands that feeling of loss is you," he stated, eyeing Khan directly, but the young man seemed to have drifted, most likely to the night that forever altered his childhood.

"I don't know how your father kept it out that she was pregnant, but he did. There was a lot of things he did that has helped me get a new trial, but I wanted you to hear from me that I'm innocent of murder, but guilty of adultery. I knew your mother was with Ronald, but she never loved him, only me, and I only loved her." Kalid finished watching a myriad of emotion play across Khan's face. He wasn't sure if he was upset, in disbelief, crestfallen or just done. So, he remained quiet and let it all soak in.

"So, you are kin to the Byse family, but Ne and Kisha don't know you? You're saying the night my mother was murdered, not only did my father kill her, but he killed the baby she was carrying? He did this because you were her first love, you all rekindled your love, but she was married to Ronald. Apparently unhappily, and sought a divorce only to die at his hands?" he recounted robotically.

"Yes. I didn't want to put all this on you, especially after Kisha's death, but you deserve the truth, and that's it. I never lifted a hand to your mother, not even when she was pregnant by another, and not when she married Ronald and had you. I was more than willing to accept every child that came from that marriage because I knew they were of her, and I didn't care. I still don't. I'm here for you, Khan. When and if you are ever ready to have me in your life. The kind of love your mother and I had was rare. Due to us being so young and inexperienced, we made mistakes. Anyway, I'm a different man now. After it happened, I was broken, my soul was bruised. I wanted revenge, but I prayed, and Nina came to see me all the time to pray with me. It was her guidance and faith that led me to accept Christ and I forgave your father and his goons for their wickedness."

Khan shook his head. "If my dad killed my mother, why does he hate black people? My entire life, I thought he felt that way because you killed my mother," Khan replied.

"Because your mother loved me. I'm what his people call an abomination, half-white, half-black, but your father despised the day I was conceived. That night he found out the child she carried belonged to me and not him, hate seized him and never let go. It was that malevolence in his heart that helped him justify killing your mother, your sibling and setting me up. Maybe he was set up to fail as his father was born and bred into the Klan mentality. He was high up in the leadership. It was his hate that killed him, and if your father doesn't stop, he'll meet the same fate. God will only allow so much for so long," Kalid answered.

Khan nodded, but words left him momentarily. He avoided Kalid's desperate stare and looked around the visitation area to relieve the mounting pressure. His eyes bucked nearly out of his head when he saw a familiar sight. Matan was visiting an inmate as well.

"What's wrong, Khan?" Kalid could immediately feel the shift in the air. Something had caught Khan's attention, and by the flexing of his jawline, it wasn't good.

"Nothing, I just thought I saw someone I knew," he replied with a frown on his face.

Kalid followed his gaze and inwardly chuckled. "That's Magnus talking to his son, Matan. Nina informed me that you are currently dating Matan's ex."

"You've been misinformed. We're not dating, we're courting. Look, Kalid, I appreciate you reaching out to me, sharing this information. I need to process everything and I'll be in touch," Khan replied as he stood up. He was well over six feet tall and now felt six inches.

"The trial will be happening near the end of the year, I think. I'd like your support."

Khan didn't reply, he just turned to leave.

* *

"Dad, I'm telling you Ma done lost her mind for real. I don't know what Grayling said to her, but she's depressed and quiet. Like, I can't even be mad at her anymore. She looks pitiful and defeated. I've never seen her like this. It's like all the wind has been sucked out her sails."

"Matan, I'on know either. She'll be a'ight. What 'bout you and dis baby business? Is da baby yours?"

"Royce ignoring everybody, so I don't know who the daddy is. I went to Grayling and Royale to apologize and get my girl back and she is stepping out on me with a white dude. Like, I get I hurt her, but you're switching races, hugging and making goo-goo eyes at this man like y'all deep in love. I know for a fact he didn't put in the work I did."

"Son, he also didn't cheat on her with her momma, so there's dat. You feel me? Now, leave dat girl alone. Don't be some obsessive stalker like yo' momma. That ain't a good look."

Matan nodded, but he didn't like his father throwing that back in his face or the shade. He accepted his mistake, apologized for it, repented and was never walking that road again. Now all he wanted was Royale back and to be in Grayling's good graces. That wasn't stalkerish. "Dad, I need Roy..." The rest of his comment died on his lips as he saw that man, the same one who was over at Royale's house who she was hugged up on. The rational part of his mind warned him to stay put, but the emotional side of him hungered for confrontation. What did this white boy have that he didn't? What was so much better about him that Royale had fallen for him like he was her only lifeline? He had to know. Without knowing this man, he disliked him.

Matan had stalked them for the short time they were in Virginia. Okay, so technically, his father was correct, but he didn't need to know that, and it angered him that her family had embraced this man as they once did him. The women fawned over him, even Rina, and she didn't like any male except Grayling. He narrowed his chocolate eyes and zeroed in on his enemy, his mind trying to comprehend who he could possibly be visiting in a maximum-security prison. That question remained unanswered as he observed Khan leaving.

"Boy, what is ya doing?" Magnus asked, a little concerned.

"Pop, I know that dude. He's the one who was hanging all over Royale like a Christmas ornament. Why is he here? I need to speak to him before he gets gone."

"Son, chill out. Now you's acting like your lurking momma. Leave them people alone. That boy came here to visit my celli, Kalid. Dude was wrongfully convicted and, believe it or not, he really is innocent. He wanted to reach out to Khan because it's his momma who Kalid was accused of murdering," Magnus explained.

That caught Matan's attention. "For real?"

"Real talk. Now what'chu need to do is forget all about this jealousy you harboring and let it go. If Royale will sit down and listen to you, then express your sorrow for the pain you done caused, but don't be pushing up on her, acting like you's thirsty.

You feel me? Leave that boy alone, he got enough demons to deal with. Don't be acting no fool over a girl you did wrong."

"Okay, Pop, I hear you. I'm going to get out of here. I'll visit again next month," Matan replied, knowing his father's advice went in one ear and out the other.

"Cool. I love ya."

"I love you also, Pop," Matan replied, and his father laughed.

"You be killing me with that proper talk. Stay out of trouble Matan, 'cause you don't want to end up here. I be praying for you, and I hope you pray for yourself. I'll see you next month, God willing."

Matan nodded, got up and headed down the same path of Khan, hoping they would run into each other.

* *

Khan felt, rather than saw Matan. He just had a feeling a corn-ball like Matan would try him. Honestly, this was the worst time to come at him over Royale when he was dealing with the worse kind of deception. His father had murdered his mother. He believed everything Kalid said. It all fit. It hurt him, enraged him to another level, like the calm Khan everyone knew was about to explode. He was in that *I-wish-you-would-mode*, and it looked like Matan wanted to be the wish.

"Excuse me?"

Khan slowly dragged his eyes from his iPhone. A message had just come through from Royale, and he had two missed calls, one from Nehemiah, and one from his murderous father. When he finally connected eyes with Matan, not that they were eye level. Matan was shorter than him, the mean mug he gave Khan would have made one believe he was a giant. "Yes?" Khan responded far cooler than he felt.

"You looked familiar to me. Aren't you that guy who was at my girl's house?"

He tried it. Khan chuckled like that was all he could do to keep his balled up left fist from crashing into Matan's pretty boy face. This guy was delusional. Once he stopped laughing, he turned his dark blue eyes onto Matan like a hawk accessing its prey. "I was indeed in Virginia, visiting my future wife, Royale, and her family. You know that. I guess you thought you were going to try me, but I'm not going to act out of character because I know who has Royale's heart. It's not you.

"Here is a warning, and you can thank me later for providing you one. Stay away from Royale and don't contact her. If she wants to reach out to you, fine, but know this, you had your chance and you blew it. If you come for my lady, disrespect her, or make her feel the least bit uncomfortable, you'll feel the wrath of Khan. Don't let the lack of melanin fool you; it'd be dangerous to underestimate me.

"I love my lady, and there isn't anything I wouldn't do to protect her from anyone. So, lobster walk yourself back to your car and never make the mistake of approaching me again. Unlike you, I'm new to this Christian walk and won't hesitate to smite a gnat like you." Khan glared at him, his words strong, but his voice even and non-lethal, yet they had the effect necessary to make Matan think twice.

Neither moved an inch, but Khan was completely unbothered. "You can go now. I have to get back to Royale," Khan added, then turned around and got into his truck as if Matan was never there. He started up his truck and backed up.

As soon as he was away from the prison, he banged his steering wheel. The pain hit him hard. He wanted to take his bare hands and crush his father, but that wasn't him. He was never a man of violence, but he knew this situation could alter that. His heartbeat increased and sweat poured down his face like a waterfall, making his hand slippery. If his father had murdered his own wife, what would stop him from murdering Royale? Did he love her enough to let her go to ensure her safety? He was too upset to see Royale now, so he reached for his phone and called Nehemiah.

Chapter 13

Matan pulled up at his mother's house, his mind still replaying what Khan had said to him, though it had pissed him off at the time. While he was on the flight back to Virginia, he did something he hadn't done in a while. He read his Bible, and he prayed not for him and Royale to get back together, but for healing, forgiveness, and enlightenment. The saved man in him knew he needed to apologize to Khan and Royale. Additionally, he and Grayling needed to have a real conversation. He knew from the way Grayling had welcomed him that day when he looked like a deranged madman that there was still something salvageable in their relationship. He needed to humble himself, and if he were indeed the father of Royce's child, then he would do all in his power to do right.

Nodding his head to confirm that, he parked his car and exited. He tried calling his mother, after making a complete fool of himself like his father had told him not to do, but she never answered. He decided to stop by and see how she was doing.

Apparently, there was something about the Chastain family that was kryptonite to his family. As he started toward the house, the hair on the back of his neck started to rise, and his body tensed up. He stopped and looked around but saw nothing out of the ordinary. Still, that warning feeling in his body hadn't eased, and he padded toward his mother's door, pulling out his key at the same time.

Once he entered the house, he didn't notice anything off, so he called out for Roslyn. She didn't respond. He went to the kitchen, but she wasn't there, so he went to every room on the first floor and found them empty. A feeling of anxiety arose in him, but he clamped it down and jogged upstairs, thinking she was probably taking a shower or resting. When he arrived at her bedroom, the door was closed. He sighed. She was sleeping, but he still wanted to speak to her. He opened the door and found her laid diagonally upon the bed.

"Ma, wake up," he called out as he ambled toward her, but she didn't respond. Matan tapped her to assist her in waking, but nothing. That was strange because she was a light sleeper. He shook her, and that's when an empty pill bottle rolled onto the floor. Matan's anxiety went to full-blown agony. He froze momentarily. He began shouting his mother's name but to no avail. He ran to her phone, forgetting his own cell phone was in his pocket and dialed 911. Just as he was connected to the operator, he saw a piece of paper folded on the nightstand. While he gave the operator the information she asked for, he also retrieved the paper.

"Sir, is she breathing?"

"No, I don't think so."

"Check, and if she isn't, then start compressions. I'll walk you through it. Just calm down and know that the ambulance is on its way."

He did as he was told and his mother wasn't breathing. Only God knew how long she had been out, and for the first time, he noticed how cold she felt, how clammy her skin was, and tears watered his face. No matter what his mother did or didn't do, she was his mom and she held him down as a single parent. She didn't deserve to leave like this.

A lifetime of mistakes fast-forwarded through his mind. "Breathe, Ma, please breathe. I'm sorry for being upset with you, for not being the son I should have been, and for allowing myself to get caught up in so much mess. I love you, Ma. Don't leave me, please." Then he started talking to God. "God, I need You, we need You. Whatever made her feel like she had to do this, please let me take her cup. Take me instead. All I've done is make a mockery of Your Word, but God, don't take her from me. Not like this, God, not like this." He wept; the operator long forgotten. Finally, the EMS arrived and took over, shoving Matan out of the way. He was still praying.

* *

Life was never easy, but then again, God never said it would be. It sure felt like Royale and Khan had been kidnapped into a Texas twister. Life was happening so fast, and they seemed to be bombarded with adversity after adversity. Royale sensed that Khan needed a break, and she knew she did as well.

Royale had originally planned to take Khan to Overlook Rock Trail, knowing it was a place of solace for him, but he was in another place mentally and had yet to talk to her. Feeling a bit out of place and still reeling from the loss of her friend Kisha and the news that Everleigh was Rina's bio-sister, she excused herself from the room and headed to the room she had called her own. Once she arrived, she began to pack a bag. She needed to head back to Virginia and deal with her vessel and ex. It was time to have a mature conversation—no running, no yelling, just understanding and forgiving. She could do that. She needed to do that, and then, she was coming back to West Virginia to help Khan. If he let her.

She feared if he stayed silent for much longer, they would drift. She had no intention of losing him. Whatever happened in that visiting room between him and Kalid, she could only speculate since he felt it necessary to shut her out. Though she tried not to show it, the fact that he felt he couldn't trust her hurt deeper than she cared to admit. Sighing annoyingly, she completed her task, and her cell phone began to ring. She looked down, and it was her father. For some reason, her spine stiffened and goose bumps appeared on her skin.

"Daddy, what's wrong?"

There was hesitation in his voice, but after a second, he spoke. "Honey, I know there's a lot happening in West—"

"Dad, no preamble, just give it to me straight. Is it Royce?" She could hear him let out a sigh on the other end. It was as if he were debating about what to say. "Dad?" she prompted, doing her best to hide her irritation. She could feel her pulse rate increasing, her skin beginning to burn with worry. It had to be Royce, what had she done now?

"It's Roslyn. Matan arrived home earlier today and found her unresponsive. I debated telling you, only because you have so much going on with Kisha's passing and Khan meeting his mother's accused murderer. I just didn't want to add more stress."

"Oh, my goodness. Is she okay?" Part of her was thankful it wasn't Royce, but she loved Sister Roslyn as well, and she was concerned.

"We don't know a lot right now."

"I'm coming home. I was coming before you called me, but I feel more of an urgency now. Something happened at the prison when Khan went to visit Kalid. I'm scared for him. I'm praying for him, but I'm scared I'll lose him I don't know what to do," she honestly replied.

"Royale, are you running again?" Her father's voice hinted at concern and not accusation. She was known to pull a Speedy Gonzales anytime she felt she was in mental overload, but she was no longer pulling those stunts. She faced her fears, no matter how severe they were.

"No, not this time, not anymore. I was coming home to finally deal with Royce and Matan. It's time to reconcile and move forward. God really put that on my heart. It has gone on long enough. Also, I've scheduled a phone conference with Trinity Hall to get our side of the story out so we can control the narrative. Lastly, it's time to get these braces off, then I'm coming back here to help Khan in any way I can, but no more running. You have my word on that."

"Thank goodness. I'm glad to hear that. You've really grown a lot, Royale, and I'm proud of you. Have you had any problems out of Khan's father?"

"No, sir. All has been quiet."

"Okay, let me know your expected time of arrival and I'll be there to pick you up. Sweetheart, I'm proud of you. I'm praying for you and Khan. As always, I'm here if you need me."

"Thank you, Daddy. I'll send you my travel itinerary."

"Bye, sweetheart." The two hung up, and Royale smiled. She put her phone up and removed her travel bag off the bed.

She felt a tingle go up her spine; it was like an invisible touch. There was only one person who could touch her without physically touching her. She quickly pivoted and bumped into Khan, and her body instantly reacted. He was her homeostasis.

He reached out his massive hands to prevent her from bouncing off him, and before she knew it, he was enfolding her into him. Her body voluntarily molded into him and tears prickled her eyelids. She slowly closed them and inhaled his scent, imprinting it into her brain. She felt his callous fingers massaging her scalp, something she never allowed in the past by friends or her ex, but with Khan, it relaxed her inner being.

"I'm sorry for scaring you, Honey Drop. It wasn't my intention to shut you out, but the information I received took me to a dark and sunken place. The more I thought about it, the more it enraged me. I reached out to Ne to help me navigate through those feelings. I didn't want to bring that back to you," he expressed, his voice strong and calm.

She nodded, and they mutual put space between them, but just enough to gaze into each other's eyes. "You once told me you'd take my brokenness and we'd heal together. Have I made you feel as if you can't bring me your brokenness? I want us, Khan. I want us despite my past and yours. My mother's mistakes aren't a reflection of me, just like your father's mistakes aren't a reflection of you. I don't need you to protect me from your dark moments. I need you to trust me enough to know that if you fall, my hands will be outstretched to lift you up. If you feel like darkness is drowning you, then I'll be your life jacket shining under God's everlasting light, but what I'll never do is abandon or betray you. Trust me with your worst, I can handle it. I love you too much to lose you. Wherever we go from here, we go together. If you aren't ready to share what you and Kalid discussed, I respect that," she told him as she cupped his face in her hands. Then she stood on her tippy toes and kissed the tip of her nose. Her thumbs caressed his cheeks, prompting him to showcase his million-dollar dimples. His hands came up and covered hers.

"I don't know how you do it, Honey Drop, but you root yourself deeper into my heart and my soul every day. I always find another reason to adore you. I love you, Royale, and you're right, I trust you. I was just under an overload of emotions and was unsure of how to deal. I wanted to confront Ronald today, but then I overheard your conversation. Are we headed back to Virginia?" he asked.

She placed her forehead on his chest and quieted for a moment. Then, she took a deep breath and explained to him about Matan's mother and her plans to make peace with her family so she could move on. "Khan, when this is all over, I'm taking you to Canada so you can show me where your mother loved to hike. I promise I won't pack the entire house," she teased, attempting to lighten up the sorrowful situation.

He chuckled. "You're always so thoughtful. What about graduate school?"

"I've decided to take a year off. There's a lot to be done back in Virginia with my father's church and family. I have my non-profit to work on, plus Rina will be attending Oxford since she's a Rhodes Scholar and I want to be around if she needs my guidance. Most of all, you and I need time together," she replied.

"Are you sure?" he asked as he dropped his forehead down to touch hers.

"God and I had a long talk, and I'm sure. We need to get you packed up, and maybe you can convince Nehemiah to come with us as well."

Khan nodded, kissed her forehead, and then turned to leave. Her eyes followed the path he took and she quietly thanked God for allowing Khan to be hers. She placed her hand over her heart and smiled.

* *

Matan was a mess. If Grayling hadn't answered when he called, he might have been in ICU like his mother. He debated telling Magnus because he didn't want to upset his father. God forbid if she didn't make it, he would be parentless.

"Breathe, Tan, Ms. Roslyn is going to be fine. You see all these people in here praying for her." Fontaine's voice interjected into his thoughts. He nodded, but the words failed to penetrate, though he was thankful all his boys had come. Fontaine had put out the call, bringing all three of them to the hospital. At least this time, the media wasn't camped out front.

"Matan."

He glanced up, saw Grayling and quickly stood. The boy in him wanted to hug Grayling, implore his forgiveness and plead for mercy. The boy in him wanted Grayling to tell him his mother would come back to him. But, the man in him was too terrified to move. It was as if Grayling sensed his need and his fear. Being the man Matan so desperately wanted to be, Grayling pulled him up to his feet and embraced him. Tears began to fall before Matan could even think. They were tears of anguish from the betrayal he had committed against the two people who cared so much about him. He cried for his mother and it broke his heart that she felt so lonely that she thought ending her life was better than living it.

"She's not going to leave you, Matan. God still hears you. Don't allow sin to disrupt your prayer, your belief and your knowledge of who God is. None of us are perfect, and we all fall short. Stop attacking yourself over the past and stay present. God is I AM, not I WAS, or I WILL BE. Stay where He is and know that I forgive you and I still love you, Matan. Forgive me for my treatment of you, but I'm here for as long as you need me."

With trembling lips and a heart beating and thumping faster and harder than a herd of scared zebras, Matan pulled away and stared at Grayling in awe and humility. "You've been a father to me and I betrayed you in the worse way. Whatever angry thoughts you've harbored were of my creation, and I'm sorry a million times over. My actions were selfish and not a representation of you, Bishop. I wish with all my heart I could erase the pain I caused. I'll be scarred a lifetime for the agony I caused you and Royale. You both have loved me in a way I never deserved. However, if this is the beginning of healing, then, Bishop Grayling, I forgive you forever and always. I'm forever sorry for the sins I've committed against you. Thank you for again showing me what it means to be a man of God and not a man of Men. You're still the man I pray to God to become.

"I know the relationship we once had will never be again, and that's on me, but I love you, Bishop Chastain. I love your daughter. It's because of that love, I understand my time with her is over, but I pray that not now, but one day I can be friends with you all again," Matan tearfully pleaded.

"It can start now." Royale's angelic voice floated through the air.

Hearing her voice was like manna to his crumbling heart. Matan turned slowly, his face dressed in tears, his eyes red and blurry, but he saw her as clear as day. There she stood, beautiful, with that kind expression on her face, hope in her eyes, her hair freely hanging down her back, and her smile. That beacon of light drew him to her. "I'm sorry, Royale. It's like I saw my life when I saw my mother lying unresponsive. I felt the pain and despair I caused you and Grayling. I never meant for things to go as far as they did and I'm sincerely sorry." He swallowed hard and looked at Khan. A man he wanted to hate but had to respect because Khan did what he failed to do: he recognized the wonderful woman Royale was. "Khan, I apologize for how I approached you in West Virginia. It was immature and careless. I had no right. If you could find it in your heart to forgive me, I would appreciate it."

"Done. I forgive you, man. I'll leave you and Royale to talk," Khan offered, then kissed Royale before sauntering off with Grayling to give the pair some privacy.

"Matan, I'm sorry for how I've treated you. I was hurt. I was in agony, but as time has progressed, so have I. You made a mistake, just like we all do. I can see that you are sincere in your apology. I accept it. I forgive you. We're friends, which is why I'm here. I'm here to support you and your mother. Hopefully, we can end this mess. My dad's right, stop beating yourself up about the past and stay present. I'll do my best to be the friend you deserve. From this day forward, I won't bring up your past. It's over. I know you might be the father of my sister or brother, but I don't see that as bad. However, the chips may fall, you'll have my support."

"Thank you, Royale. I needed to hear that from you and Grayling."

"Good, now let's pray for your mother's recovery," she told him and then motioned for her father to come over. Grayling had everyone get up, hold hands and bow their heads, and he led them in prayer. Matan let the tears fall at the love and support he was being shown. In his pocket, the letter burned his pocket. He hadn't told anyone he had found it or what it said. He vowed to God to be a better man, so a part of him didn't want to share the contents of the letter because it would only add fuel to the fire. At the end of the day, the most rotten person in this equation wasn't present—Royce.

Chapter 14

Grayling entered Roslyn's hospital room. He convinced Matan to take a break from holding vigil at her bedside, but only after Matan shared with him the suicide letter Roslyn had left behind. It broke his heart because Royce had been a part of it. Shaking his head, he sat at Roslyn's side and placed his hand over hers and prayed for healing of her mind, body, and spirit. She was really going through it. He felt like a part of that was his fault. Though Roslyn went about it the wrong way, she was still in love with him. Just as he finished the prayer, her hand moved. He opened his eyes to see her staring back at him in confusion.

Knowing that she must be thirsty, he picked up the plastic container filled with ice water and let her drink, but she shook her head no.

"Why are you here?" she stuttered out, her voice hoarse from underuse.

"I'm your pastor and your friend, why wouldn't I be here?" he asked.

"I mean, I was supposed to die. I can't even do that right," she complained.

"Roslyn, talk to me. Matan found the letter and he shared it with me, but what I don't understand is why you felt this was the answer."

He saw her struggling to answer, and he gently patted her shoulder, letting her know she was in a safe space, and he wasn't going to judge her. "Speak when you are ready. I'm not here to judge you. I'm just here to help you."

Tears rolled down her cheek, which sort of surprised him. Roslyn wasn't a crier. It just wasn't her thing. She was the kind of person that if you hurt her, she just hurt you worse, but she never allowed her enemy to see her weak. "This is all my fault."

"How?"

She took a deep breath, but by the pained look on her face, he knew it hurt her to move that way. She'd been out for a while, so he knew her body was stiff. She forced her body to turn toward him, and she gazed into his eyes, unwavering. She swallowed, hard. He actually heard it and reached for her water to again offer her a drink. She accepted, then put her hand up to signal she was done.

"Grayling," she paused, he assumed to collect her thoughts before speaking her truth. "Grayling, when we were back in school, I adored you. Maybe it was unhealthy the obsession I had with you, but honestly, you were the only good in my life. I've always been prone to depression because of my family situation. My father had long abandoned the family and my mother was in the streets, but I didn't care because I had you. I finally had someone who wanted me and I latched onto that like a parasite. Then I met Royce, but that was before I knew she was wealthy and uppity. She seemed to be like me, both broken and seeking someone to understand. We clicked, which was why I trusted her enough to be around you.

"I knew she was being abused, she told me and I felt bad for her. I was willing to get some of the street boys to handle her situation, but then she betrayed me. She stole your heart, and you let her. That's when she started strutting her labels and looking like a supermodel, and I couldn't compete. She played that innocent, good girl act so good. I believed it. I wanted revenge after you broke up with me. I knew about the old dude who was messing with her, so after I saw how you were with her and that you weren't checking for me, I put a plan into action. It took some time, but I was patient. I set up a robbery, it went bad, and Magnus took the fall because I was pregnant.

"Then I followed you and watched in the distance as you and Royce built up your church. I reached out to you when I had Matan, and Royce hated it, but I threatened to tell about her old life and she let it be. Then, Matan and Royale grew up together and started dating. I thought that would be enough and I would still have you in my life. What I didn't know was that your wife was plotting her own revenge. If she were caught with Matan, then not only would you get rid of my son, but also me. This was her payback. She never expected you to react how you did, or at least that was what she said when she barged into my home. Then, she threatened to expose me. Add that to the rejection you handed me at your home, which, by the way, she saw, which was why she was pissed at me. Then my son was upset with me, and even Magnus, who has the patience of British guards, laid into me, and I just gave in.

"I didn't think anyone would care if I died. I know you're only here out of duty. I appreciate it, but I believe it's best if you go your way and I go mine. Being around you isn't healthy for me. I'm not strong enough right now. I always wanted to mean something to you, and I know I went about it all wrong, but it was never to intentionally hurt you. I just got caught up loving someone who can't and will never love me. I get that now. That's the story, all truth, no lie. It's all about revenge. An old school battle between myself and Royce that has impacted our children, put a good man in prison and nearly ruined a marriage. I apologize for what I've done, and hopefully, you'll forgive me, but right now, I can't be around you."

Grayling sat back in the chair, stunned, perplexed and empathetic. He didn't know that Roslyn had invested so much into their high school relationship. He felt responsible. He got with Royce and all thoughts of anyone else never crossed his mind. Here was Roslyn, hurting so badly she thought death was the answer. She surprised him by telling him she couldn't be around him.

"Does Magnus know any of this?"

"He finally put it together, but he has never called me out on it.

Magnus isn't that kind of man. He doesn't do petty."

"He's a good man, Roslyn."

"I know. He's far too good for me. I should be in prison, not him."

"Maybe we can get him out. I'll talk with the General. My father-in-law has a lot of pull, and that man has done a lot of time."

She just nodded. It seemed to him she had drifted into another place. "Rossi, I'm going to leave as you requested. I do forgive you, and I sincerely apologize for how my past actions have impacted you. I never wanted this, ever." He got up and leaned over and kissed her forehead.

He waited for a moment to see if she would respond, but she didn't. He understood. He pulled her blanket up, prayed over her, and then left the room. All this destruction was because he had broken one woman's heart to be with another broken woman. In the end, it was his daughter who suffered, and she was completely innocent. He prayed to God that she and Khan would find happiness because he did not want Royale to be hurt anymore.

* *

Royce pulled up at the hospital, and she had her camera crew with her. Who knew her little threat would cause poor Roslyn to end up in the hospital? Didn't she warn that woman she wasn't the one to mess with? Royce saw her enter the home she shared with Grayling and she peeked in the windows and saw her trying to seduce her man. She had to pay for that, which was why she threatened to tell not only Matan, but the world about who Roslyn used to be.

It had been three days since Roslyn had been hospitalized, and according to Royce's spies, she had finally woken up a much weaker, less abrasive woman. Oh well, it was time for her to bow down and bow out. Royce sashayed into the hospital as if she owned it. She knew they wouldn't permit her cameras in the ICU, which was why she had one on her necklace.

Once she arrived at the waiting room, she noticed her daughter and an extremely handsome white man sitting beside her, holding her hand. Interesting, she silently thought to herself. She glided over to the pair, who seemed to be reading the scripture. Something inside of her became dark. It angered her that her daughter, who had singlehandedly destroyed her marriage by telling Grayling of her past failings, was now enraptured by a new man.

How dare she be giddy, glowing and grateful as if the Matan situation never happened. Where was that mean girl who was in her hospital room? That was what made ratings go sky high. Had she been smart, she would have had cameras rolling then. Well, she was prepared now.

It did infuriate her to see Royale supporting Roslyn. How dare her daughter be here for Roslyn and not be supportive of her? Shaking the feeling of disloyalty, she put on her game face. It was time for retribution, and they all would pay. That was what she was calling her new reality show, *The Retribution of Royce.*

"Royale," Royce's perky, breathy voice called out.

Her daughter did a double take, but the disappointment she knew she would find in Royale's eyes wasn't there. Even Royale's body language was comforting, compelling even, throwing Royce a bit off her game. She almost stopped in her tracks, almost. She was prepared for animosity, a fight, some sort of rancor, yet Royale greeted her with kindness.

"Royce, how are you?" Royale asked politely.

Uh, so there was some level of anger as she addressed her as Royce and not mama. "Who is this handsome gentleman?"

"Hello, ma'am, I'm Khan Masterson, Royale's significant other," he greeted, standing up.

She lifted a brow and slowly, her eyes accessed Khan from head to toe. He was unbelievably handsome. Maybe Royale had a bit of her mother in her. Physically, he was nothing like Matan.

"It seems my daughter has been keeping secrets. It's nice to meet you as well, significant other Khan." Then she turned her attention to Royale. "Can I at least have a hug?" Royce watched as her daughter got up and walked over to her. Royce widened her arms, and Royale allowed her to embrace her. To Royce's surprise, Royale deepened the embrace and then she whispered in Royce's ear.

"Mother, it isn't me who keeps secrets, it's you. I know what you did. We all do. I know you threatened Roslyn about something she did years ago, something she meant to use to hurt you, but she hurt herself instead. You preyed on her weaknesses. She was wrong, but so were you. You've been wrong for a long time. God won't let it continue," she expressed, her unseen hand rubbing up and down Royce's back, causing Royce to stiffen, but she remained silent as her daughter continued to speak. "I know you came here to expose us as part of your revenge reality show, but I'm granting you what you have never offered another. I forgive you, and despite all your cruelty, I love you. It's because of that forgiveness and love that I'll continue to pray the hell out of your spirit." There was a pregnant pause and Royce began to push away, but her daughter held her tightly. "Oh, and I saw the look you gave Khan. I strongly suggest you not attempt to come for him. I let you have Matan, but the demons will ice skate in Hell before I let you near Khan. I'm a woman of God, but I'm still a woman, and God isn't done with me yet. Try me again if you want to, mother, but I'm not a scared little girl anymore. I'm all grown." Then she pulled away and kissed her mother on both cheeks. "I pray one day you'll find peace and seek the path and purpose God created you for because this isn't it, Mother, it really isn't." She winked at Royce and then went back to Khan.

Just like that, the wind went out of Royce's sails. Royce was left speechless. Her daughter was both polite and petty, sanctified and savage, and threw shade and Scripture all at once. With the grace that only Royale could exude, she properly scolded Royce. A part of her was upset, but also proud. Royale really had found her backbone, and she wasn't backing down. She might just keep this new man she had.

However, one thing did bother her. How had her plan been soiled before it ever came to fruition? "Royce." She knew that deep baritone as well as she knew her own voice.

With extra drama that she had perfected over the years, she pivoted and came face to face with her husband. His molasses-colored skin glowed. His eyes didn't travel up or down the contour of her body; instead, he kept his eyes steady on hers. There was no resentment. The bags that once attached his face were gone, his appearance seemed lighter, the strained stress lines that had scarred his face were replaced by smooth skin and back was his mustache and beard combo. He looked incredibly handsome, strong and statuesque. He was reminiscent of the young man she had fallen for decades ago. She closed her eyes and inhaled his scent of African musk and Egyptian oil. So many good memories followed, but then she came back to reality.

"Grayling." It came out as a question and answer all in one.

"We need to have a conversation, Royce. There'll be no shouting, manipulating or lying. You won't attempt to use your past abuse as an excuse, and you won't distract me with unfounded allegations. Now, I'm sure Royale made you aware that we know about your devious plans to seek revenge, however, that won't be happening now or ever. Come with me and take off the cameras."

She stood stunned, but the look in Grayling's eyes and the warning in his voice took away all the strength she thought she had. He wasn't about to entertain her, and she had played her last hand. So, she assumed Marc had sold her out. That had to be the only way they knew what she had planned. "I'm sorr—"

Grayling cut her off. "Let's go. There's no need for phony apologies. We all know you aren't sorry. You've never been, but you are broken, and since you're still my wife, it's my duty to do everything in my power to restore you back to you."

She didn't reply, she just took off the hidden camera and placed her hand in the proffered hand of her husband. Then she allowed him to escort her out of the hospital, her evil plan thwarted maybe for a moment, or maybe forever.

* *

A few hours later, Khan and Royale were sitting on Ma Gwendolyn's patio holding hands and watching Royale's mentee, January, her siblings and Rina swim in the pool. Khan wanted to spend some alone time with Royale. Since they had been together, there was constantly something happening and them finding alone time was difficult. It seemed this was as close as they could get for now.

"Khan, I know I've said it before, but again, thank you for how you've been with Matan. I still can't get over him approaching you back when you went to see Kalid. I appreciate how you handled the situation then and are handling it now."

He turned to her and offered her a sad smile. "I know what it's like to not have a mom. That fear and uncertainty can corrode everything. He just needed reassurance. I really hold no hard feelings against him. If I lost you, I'd be pissed too.

"I'm glad his mother survived. I wouldn't wish the death of a parent on anyone, especially when it's the only one you have. Matan apologized about the incident, and we've talked since. I know he's learned his lesson and I'm just thankful you were able to get the closure you needed."

She nodded. That she did. It felt like she had lost a load the moment she forgave Matan and her mother. Their actions wounded her, but the wound was healed, with no scars left behind. That was all God's doing. When it first happened, she couldn't see through the fog, but now, she could see a future and that gave her peace.

"So, the way you went off on your mom, that was hot. You were like stay away from my fine, good looking, super handsome, nothing is better than him, man," he boasted.

Royale threw her head back and guffawed until tears drowned her. "You are so too much. I can see Canton has rubbed off on you. I didn't say all of that."

"Honey Drop, it was implied," he teased, before lifting her out of her lounge chair and placing her on his lap. "You know I'm at my happiest when I'm close to you. Even with everything that has happened and may happen, you are my calmness and my happiness. I'm forever grateful to God that He loves me enough to gift me you," he told her, his hands framing her face.

She blushed but kissed the inside of his hand. He could be so romantic with his words, and she was so glad he wasn't the kind of man who was afraid to share his feelings. "These are my favorite moments. I never get tired of hearing how you feel about me. You make everything feel new. I feel so connected to you that it's scary, but I can't imagine life without you, and I often wonder how I made it before you. I never knew how much I needed you until I found you. I'm not afraid to tell you that. The old me would've been, but we've been through a lot in a short period of time. Most relationships would break under the pressure we've survived. We're stronger now. I'm thankful every single day for you, my love."

"Okay, enough of the love speech. Good grief. Do you two ever give it a break? Didn't Antwon tell you to keep Royale off your lap? I'm going to tell it!" Rina teased.

"Stop being a hater, Czarina Gail, or I'll tell Canton on you," Khan joked back, causing Rina to turn fire engine red. She gave Khan a glare that would stop a man in his tracks, but Khan was laughing too hard to notice.

"I don't care if you call him."

"Okay," Khan replied as he pulled out his cell phone.

"Khan, you better not or I'll put you back on the block list," Rina threatened.

"I thought you didn't care."

"Khan," Royale warned, knowing these two would go back and forth all day if she permitted it.

"Fine, I won't call."

Royale watched in amusement as Rina visibly relaxed. Royale was sure then that she might be a little interested in Canton, but due to her issues with her father, men really did scare her. It still shocked her that Everleigh Jacobs was Rina's bio-sister. The two couldn't be more different; the only thing they had in common was their eye color.

"Truce, Rina?" Khan asked.

"Truce," she replied and then rounded up the kids, leaving Royale and Khan alone.

The pair was silent for a while, but Khan noticed Royale was picking at her hands, something she did when there was something on her mind, and she wasn't sure how to express herself. "What's the matter?"

"Not well, I don't want you to go back to West Virginia. I feel like it's the quiet before the storm and I don't want anything to happen. Currently, Nehemiah isn't there, he's down in Texas with Canton, so who'll have your back? I can't come until later. I just don't feel good about you leaving and not having someone with you."

He nodded his head in understanding. He lifted her chin so they could make direct contact. "I won't be alone, God is with me everywhere, even to the ends of the earth. I'm not leaving until after your father's sermon. Don't go worrying about anything, instead, pray about everything," he lectured.

"Well, somebody has been doing their Bible study," she stated. Then she started to tickle his stomach to distract him from their serious conversation.

He laughed, but easily overpowered her and pulled her into a hug. "I'll be fine."

"You better be, or you'll deal with pissy me and it ain't nothing pretty."

"I beg to differ. Everything about you is pretty."

She just laughed and fell into his arms.

"Hey, didn't you promise me Starbucks?"

"Yes."

"So, let's drop off these kids, and have a little Starbucks date."

Chapter 15

The smell of gasoline and fire serenaded Ronald's nostrils. It was like a high to him. He was watching the Byse family home church burn. The church that stole his son from him. If this didn't get his son's attention to let him know he wasn't playing, then his next move would. If not, he would just kidnap his son. At the end of the day, Khan belonged to him.

"That sure is pretty," Hoss commented, watching the blaze tear through the church.

"It is. I bet that'll get Khan's attention. So, have you heard from Strom? I tried to get into contact with Everleigh, you know, just to check on her, but her phone wasn't on."

"Nah, I ain't heard from neither of them. You thinking something off?" Hoss queried, as they heard the fire truck siren in the distance.

"Could be. Everleigh said her dad didn't take it so well when he found out. I guess because that Byse chick was friends with that abomination he created. I just wanted her to know that she had our support. I swear Strom was never the same after marrying that muddy. I know it was for a greater cause, but he should have just gone and killed himself. He can never wash that black disease off."

"What about Khan? You think that about him too?"

"No. One thing I know about my boy is that he respects women, even them others, so he ain't doing that with her. He's all about marriage and being with one woman."

"Seriously?"

"Yeah, unless he met someone in college. The boy just different like that, which is why I've dedicated my life to make him tough. Oh, did I tell you Lorelai called me earlier today?"

"Nah, you didn't tell me about that. That's another waste. I can't believe she married outside of her race. I know your daddy is turning over in his grave."

"It's a shame. She asked me if I killed Kisha Byse and I was like who have you been talking to that would make you think I murdered that gal. It seems Canton was running his mouth to his dad, who felt it necessary to phone my sister. She's talking about coming for a visit. I told her she and her pet monkey weren't welcomed in the state of West Virginia, let alone my house."

Hoss let out a howl of laughter. "What'd she say after that?"

"She hung up. I swear I done been cursed with a soft son and a stupid sister. What they see in them cursed people is beyond me. All them darkies do is bring crime and disease. They're like a freaking rat infestation that needs to be exterminated."

"I agree with you on that. Let's start exterminating," Hoss added.

They would, real soon.

*   *

Khan awoke to his phone ringing. He muffled out a few words before throwing off his covers and reaching for his cell phone. He didn't even check the ID. "Hello?"

"Khan Masterson?"

"This is he speaking. Who is calling?"

"Hello, Khan, this is Desiree, the nurse from Dr. Talabi's office. We've been trying to contact your father, but have been unable to do so, and he had you down as his contact person who we can share his medical information with. It's imperative he comes in for treatment. The earlier we start, the better chance we have of getting him into remission."

Khan sat all the way up. "What exactly is wrong with him? I know he had OA, but this sounds like something else."

"It is. Your father has several medical issues due to his drinking. Can you come in so we can discuss it?"

"No, I'm out of state, so just tell me what you can. Is he dying?" Because if he was, then that was just him reaping what he sowed.

"His drinking is destroying his kidneys and liver, but we discovered after his complaints that he has liver cancer."

Khan wasn't surprised. The old man drunk hard liquor and beer for as long as he could remember. "I see. Who did you say you were again?" He needed to verify that his father wasn't trying to lure him back to West Virginia under false pretenses. He didn't trust his father.

"I'm Desiree, the nurse. Look, if you and your father could come in so we can start treatment, that would be great. I'm sure you and he both will have questions, which Dr. Talabi can answer if you come back in."

"Okay, thank you. I'll make sure he schedules an appointment."

"We can do that now. I'm transferring you over to Judy."

While he waited, the elevator music played, but his mind was on the fact that his father was sicker than he thought. It seemed Ronald was keeping that from him.

"Khan, are you okay?" Royale's candied voice called out.

He looked up and instantly smiled. He motioned her to come into the bedroom and patted the edge of the bed for her to sit down on. She was dressed in her workout clothes, so he assumed she and Rina were about to hit up the gym, which was good because he wanted to speak to the General. He covered the phone and started to share with Royale what the PA had told him about his father. Just as she was about to question him, Judy came on the line. They made an appointment, and then he hung up.

No sooner than he put his phone down did it ring again. This time, he looked to see who it was. It was Ma Byse. She and Keith had gone out of town, so he figured they were calling to check in.

"Hey, how are you all doing?"

"Oh, Khan, I was worried sick. The deacon called and told us the church was set on fire. It's a total loss. They're sure it's arson. For some reason, I feared you were there. I know Nehemiah went to visit Canton and that he's safe, but I wasn't sure where you and Royale were. My heart just can't take losing anybody else right now."

"No, ma'am, Royale and I are in Virginia. I'm fine. Did they say who did it?" he asked, praying it wasn't his father, but knowing it was. It was just the sort of thing he would do. He burned Khan's business, so it wasn't a leap that he would burn the church he attended. His father was a murderer too. He believed Kalid when he said his father was the one who had murdered his mother. It made all the sense in the world now. He hated black people because his mother was in love with a black man, and he hated the Byses because they knew about it.

"I can only assume."

"Ronald," Khan deadpanned.

"I put nothing past him anymore. A person full of hatred can justify a life of sin. I believe in my heart he had my child killed. In his mind, it's a life for a life. I wasn't going to tell you, and I would never tell Nehemiah, but Ronald sent me a card after Kisha's funeral saying just that. Then he added he would torment us until you came back to him."

Khan reddened in anger. "Did you at least notify the police?"

"How? Who can we trust? He was the police once and he has pull."

"Not over everyone. Keep everything you have; I'm going to talk to someone who has more power than he does. He won't get away with this," he vowed.

"Khan, don't do anything rash."

"I won't. Royale wouldn't let me if I tried."

"Okay, then. Be safe, and keep Royale safe. I love you."

"I love you too," he replied before hanging up.

"What happened?" Royale asked, panicking.

"Honey Drop, calm down, just breathe through it." He waited for her to calm. "So, somebody burned down the church the Byse family and I attend in West Virginia. She and I both believe it was Ronald. It's his way of communicating with me. I need to go back to West Virginia and deal with this."

"You most certainly will not. The Byse family shouldn't even return there. It's not safe. He means to do you bodily harm, and them too. Who burns a church? People who don't have the good sense to fear God, and if you don't fear God, then you're a fool and fools do anything. So, no, you can't go back," she declared, folding her arms and tilting her head to the side.

He almost grinned. She looked so adorable trying to be all tough, but it had to be done. "Royale, I have to do this. I know you don't like it, and if there were any other way to end this, I would do it. He's somehow orchestrated Kisha's death, burned a church, and Kalid told me it was my father who killed my mother. He purposefully set Kalid up to take the fall. I owe it to my mom and Kisha, who was like my sister, to defend their honor and bring justice."

Tears started to fall down her face. "He killed your mother?" she questioned, an unreadable expression appearing on her face.

"That's what Kalid said, and although I can't pull up the memory, I looked in that man's eyes, and I knew he was pouring his soul out to me. I need to finish this. I want us to get married and have children one day, but baby, I can't do that until this threat is eliminated."

"I don't want you to go. He's a killer, Khan, you aren't. If he killed your mother and helped in some way to kill Kisha, then what makes you think he won't kill you, or even me?"

"That's why I'm going. Please don't fight me on this, Royale."

She blinked back more tears, and then got up and stormed out. He called after her, but she kept moving. That action broke his heart. He fisted his hands in his hair before slamming them violently into his mattress.

After calming himself, he made a call to Canton and Nehemiah, then he showered. Once he was done, he reached out to the General. He wasn't leaving Virginia until he was sure Royale was okay, just in case this was his last time with her. He had no idea what was going to happen, but he wasn't going to let anyone hurt the woman he loved.

* *

Grayling and Matan entered Holy Trinity Inter-Faith Worship

Center together. They had invited Trinity Hall as well. They were live streaming the event. It was Royale's idea, part of her controlling the narrative. This was real television, not a scripted reality show. It was time to show a united front and to pull the church back together. Grayling was a man of his word and practiced what he preached. It took him a moment, but God had directed his path and he was ready to lead the church and deal with the mess of his wife and mentee. Tonight, was about Matan, who he felt was ready to deliver this sermon. The entire family was there to support, and that made Grayling happy.

Grayling watched like a proud father as Matan strolled up to the microphone. He was nervous, and Grayling understood why, but he admired Matan for speaking to the church members individually as well as to the board, and now to the congregation. He listened to him preach and then out of the corner of Grayling's eyes, he saw Rina walking up to the pulpit holding a basin of water. She sat it right down at his feet. He was concentrating so hard on her that he missed Matan ambling over. Before he knew it, Matan was on his knees.

"Church family, I made mistakes, I chose to sin. I sinned against a man who has been like a father to me. I sinned against a man who taught me about God, who mentored me from a boy to a teenager and then to a man. I betrayed him just as Judas betrayed Jesus. He forgave me, even though his forgiveness I don't deserve. Not only did he forgive me, but he still loves me and accepted me back into his family. If that doesn't showcase the God in him, then I don't know what does. This is truly a man of God, and I come before you today to wash his feet. Bishop Grayling, I wash your feet as an act of humility, as an apology and as a servant of Jesus Christ. Our church has gone through a difficult time, and I'm to blame for that. Today is a new day, and I pray we can overcome this transgression and love each other again." After drying off Grayling's feet, Matan turned around and faced the church again. "If you would all have me, I'd like to come back home. I confess my sins, and I implore you all for forgiveness."

"Come back home, son. We still love you," a woman shouted.

"That's right. We all sinners saved by grace," an older gentle-man added.

The entire church stood up with their arms opened to him and he wept. He felt so overcome by the Holy Spirit that his legs gave out, but Khan had come out of nowhere and held him up. "I guess we're brothers in Christ now," Khan replied, holding him up.

"So we are," Matan replied as Royale and her entire family joined him. Patty started singing her signature song, and Matan just closed his eyes, thanking God. His momma was alive, Royale and Grayling were back in his life, and most of all, God still loved him. That was all he needed. If he were the father of Royce's baby, he could handle that too because he had the support he needed now. Even Khan was growing on him.

Chapter 16

Sunday morning, Khan was sitting in church with Royale. They had just been here a few days ago when Matan recommitted himself back to God and the church. It was an eye-opening experience for Khan, and he respected Matan for doing it. Today, he was getting the full-on Bishop Grayling experience, and it was everything.

He was never the kind of person who stood up and jumped in church, but he had been on his feet the entire service. It was like God was speaking directly to him. He even let a few tears fall. His heart was heavy with emotion. Part of him hated his father for the destruction he had caused, the killing, the lying and the abuse, but then the saved Khan tried to understand that an unsaved man didn't view his actions the way a saved man did. That was where he had a problem. He wanted revenge, but then he saw the aftermath of ungodly revenge and how that destroyed families. Royce and Roslyn were a cautionary tale.

"Will you come? If you want to have God in your life, come today," Grayling called out to the congregation.

Khan didn't hesitate. He trotted the short distance and sat in the chair. He felt like God had placed a hand on him and carried him down. To his left was Matan, who smiled at him and nodded approvingly. There were also a few kids who had come to join them. When Khan glanced up, he saw Marc. He didn't know the man well, but he knew Royale and Rina weren't fans of his. So, to see him coming down to give his life to Christ was powerful. If they felt like he did, their hearts had to be on fire for God.

Out of nowhere, this powerful voice exploded into song and Khan snapped to see Royale singing. She hadn't sung for him since that night when she sang the lullaby, but that did her vocals no justice. Her voice went right through his soul. He thought Patty Royce could sing, but Royale's voice was untouchable. It was an experience to hear her sing, and Rina played the piano like her life was on the line. They were some blessed women.

"Her voice will take your breath away and bring it back," Matan whispered.

"Indeed."

"You see what God can do, family? You see how the kingdom is growing?" Bishop Grayling preached, calling the entire church to receive the newest members.

The church came down, and there were a lot of people who welcomed them with hugs, kisses, and handshakes. It was something that left Khan speechless. These people didn't know him, but here they were, embracing him, accepting him, loving him all because God loved them. How could his father, who raised him, not show him this kind of love?

When he saw the Byse family, his cousin Canton and his family, and his Aunt Lorelai, he broke down. He didn't even know they had come.

"I'm proud of you, baby. I knew one day you'd come to understand and crave this kind of love, God's love." Nina excitedly hummed, embracing him.

"I know now."

"I'm proud of you, Khan, and your mother would be too," Lorelai told him, placing her forehead on his. She looked nothing like her brother, his father. She had darker blonde hair and expressive gray eyes. "I'm glad you've found love. You deserve it," she told him before moving on.

"My brother from another mother, I've prayed for this day. I knew it was coming. You're my blood brother now," Nehemiah told him, grabbing the back his head and bringing him into a hug. "Love will always defeat hate. You have God's entire army.

Ain't nothing Ronald can do; you belong to God now."

"Thanks, Ne."

"I love you, bruh."

"I love you, too, bruh."

Nehemiah smiled and followed the path of Lorelai.

The last person to welcome him was Royale, and she had big, juicy tears in her eyes, as if she didn't know he was going to do this. "Welcome to the family. I love you."

"I love you too. Would it be inappropriate if I kissed you?"

She smacked his chest. "Yes, I'll kiss you in the car. My mentee is around here somewhere, I can't be showing out like that. We have enough issues in the church without the Bishop's daughter accosting a newly saved child of God."

He chuckled, but pulled her into an embrace and kissed her cheek. "Feel free to accost me anytime."

"Khan!" she admonished, but he didn't care. He loved her.

*　　*

KB and Lecrae's "Church Clap" played in the background as everyone, except for Royce and Roslyn, were at Gwen's house eating. They had a massive cookout, and so much to celebrate. Royale was sitting on Khan's lap, spying on Rina.

Rina was doing her best to avoid Canton, and he was doing his best to talk to her. It all had Royale a bit stumped. She hadn't spoken to Rina about it because she didn't want to make her uncomfortable, but after today, she was going to find out what was going on.

"Khan, did you explain to Canton that Rina has issues with men outside of our family and you?" she queried, turning up her lips.

"I told him," he defended, putting up his hands, showing her, he had nothing else to do with it. "I explained it just like you told me. But hey, he likes her. He's had a crush on her since you all were on that reality show. I'm sure if he goes too far, which he won't, Antwon will hem him up. Do you not see your godfather keeping an eye on them, not to mention your dad?" Khan asked.

She glanced in that direction, and sure enough, Antwon stood like a sentinel, his eyes accessing Rina and Canton. However, what caught her eye was how Ma Gwendolyn was gazing all *coo coo for cocoa puffs* at Antwon. She had the same glint in her eyes that Royale had every time she saw or thought of Khan. "Babe, do you think my aunt and godfather got something going on?"

"Honey Drop, you're late to the game. I saw that when I first came to visit. They're together."

"No," she refuted, with a perplexed facial expression as she debated Khan's statement.

"Babe, yes they are. That man won't let her go five feet away from him without him checking where she is. He can't keep his hands off her, and he practically lives at this house. Also, you've been planted on my lap since we've been here and he hasn't said a word. *Why?* Because he's too busy with Gwen. I'm telling you, they're together. There's something about you Chastain women, got men falling in love at first sight. Poor Canton and I never stood a chance, it ain't right," he teased.

"Hush up," she giggled, wrapping her arm around him.

"I'm serious. That's why we're only having sons. I think I'd be worse than the General."

She laughed out loud. "Stop. Seriously, you think they're together?"

"I know they are. I don't know why you're in denial."

Just as the words left his mouth, Antwon nodded at the DJ to stop the music, then he got everyone's attention. "Family and friends, I've wanted to do this for a long time. I've known the Chastain family since forever. Gray is my best friend, Rina and Royale are my goddaughters, we're family," he expressed, then preceded to get down on one knee. "I've loved Gwendolyn Elise Chastain for a long time." The crowd got loud and then quiet, not wanting to miss those special words. "Gwen, would you do me the honor of being my helpmate? Will you marry me?"

"Yes," Rina yelled out, causing everyone to laugh. "Sorry," she replied, turning red when everyone looked at her.

"I told you they were together," Khan whispered to Royale, who was completely enwrapped in the moment. Her mouth formed a perfect O shape, and her eyes were dancing with merriment. She, like the others, waited with bated breath for her to say yes, but it never came. Instead, she said the one word no one ever suspected. "Strom?"

That knocked Royale out of her daze and she gripped Khan tightly. "Uh oh. Lord help us all," Royale whispered.

*　*

Strom knew immediately he had interrupted something special. It wasn't his intention to do so. He had come here to warn the family of what was coming, and who. However, the stunned look on Gwen's face, the terrified look on Czarina's face, and the pained look on Royale's face let him know he was up for a battle. He barely moved an inch before Antwon, Grayling, the General and some unknown men came at him.

He raised his arms in surrender. "I mean no one any harm. I come in peace."

"You shouldn't have come at all," Eli hissed.

"I'm trying to help," Strom offered.

"Then leave. That's the only way you can help. I swear if you don't, this will not end well for you," Antwon snapped.

"Look, I get it. When I was here last, I did some unforgivable things, but Czarina is still my daughter. Believe it or not, I do care for her, Gwen and Royale, which is why I'm here," Strom defended.

He watched as Royale got up and went to comfort his daughter. He didn't think she would react so badly to seeing him. She was sobbing so hard; her body was trembling. She couldn't be consoled. That hurt him because he was the person who had caused her pain.

"Daddy, Uncle Antwon, can you make him leave? She won't calm down until he's gone. She's not ready for him," Royale explained.

Strom shook his head. He didn't know his arrival would cause this kind of upset. "Czarina, honey, I'm sorry. Please calm down," he shouted out to her.

"Don't you ever speak to her. She's not your daughter. You gave up that right when you nearly beat her mother to death. They're my family now," Antwon fumed.

"She is. Whether you like it or not, that's my daughter."

Antwon balled up his fist and prepared to take a swing, but Gwen stopped him. "Don't. The girls have seen enough violence, and so have I. I don't want this, Antwon," she implored, and he dropped his fist, wrapping his arm around her instead.

"Strom, leave. If you want to talk, we can do that elsewhere, but not here. The women aren't ready. This was a private family event that you weren't invited to at all. You're trespassing. Do yourself a favor and leave," Grayling replied, dangerously calm.

"Grayling, I didn't come here to start anything. I swear. I came here to warn you all about the rumblings in West Virginia. It was my daughter who hurt that girl, but it wasn't her fault. She just got caught up in the movement and was heavily under Ronald's influence."

"What?" several voices chorused at once. It was then he noticed Nina and Keith Byse were there, as well as their son, Nehemiah. He had seen them all on the news. In the blink of an eye, everything went into pure chaos.

Chapter 17

Royale was wrapped in Khan's arms, her tears dressing his muscled flesh. He had no idea how she could fold her body the way it currently was and be comfortable, but he didn't try to reposition her. She wasn't in a good mind space. How could she be? For the past twenty minutes, Royale had been in his arms, her crying and him attempting to soothe her, but his mind was still riveted by the confession of Everleigh's father. She was the one who had caused Kisha to wreck and then die from her injuries. What followed that admission, for lack of better wording, was the prelude to Hell. It was like WWE Royal Rumble. The backyard looked like a level five hurricane had touched down.

It was almost too much for Rina, who was now locked in her bedroom, refusing to allow anyone to enter. The General had taken Strom somewhere, Gwen was crying in her bedroom where Antwon was comforting her and Grayling was doing his best to help Rina through a closed door. How a day of peace had become this was beyond him. As soon as he could get Royale to a better place, he needed to get back to West Virginia. This had to end, and it needed to end now.

"Honey Drop, what can I do to make it better?"

"Everleigh killed Kisha because Kisha was defending me. I don't know how you can make that better, Khan. It was senseless. It's just like what happened between my mother and Roslyn. It's so parallel that it's scary. Everleigh wants you back, but you're with me, so she lashes out, Kisha defends me, but since

I'm not there for Everleigh to unleash her madness, she takes her revenge out on Kisha. Then your father... I just can't."

He didn't speak, he just caressed her back. "I have to go back and finish this. I still need to go with Ronald to the doctor's appointment. However, I'm not leaving until I know you're okay."

"Don't go, Khan. There's no reason for you to be there."

"I won't be alone. Canton and Nehemiah will come."

"I'm imploring you, don't go. I think this is all just to get you to come back so they can turn you into them. I don't trust Strom, he's one of them."

He closed his eyes and let out short breaths. He didn't want to upset her, but this had to be done. They had talked about this before. He knew the arrival of Strom had shaken Royale, Rina, and Gwendolyn the most. It was like they were reliving what he had done to them and he hadn't the heart to hurt her more. He leaned down and kissed the side of her cheek. He'd stay a little longer. His business was doing fine, and besides, Royale was what was important.

* *

Four weeks later...

Matan sat down in the proffered chair in Grayling's office. His mother was making a full recovery and was currently getting Christian counseling to deal with her issues. It was Royce who was the problem now. Although she, too, was present because Grayling had persuaded Royce to get a non-invasive prenatal DNA paternity test.

Matan was nervous because he had come to terms with what happened and he, too, was in counseling. However, he just didn't trust Royce. The last couple of months illustrated to him just how evil she could be and just how selfish she was. She seemed unusually calm, maybe because Grayling hadn't filed for divorce.

"Well, I have the results. Matan, do you want to open yours first?"

Matan nodded and picked up the envelope and slowly peeled it open. His breath quaked, but he continued. He glanced through and then let out a sigh. "I'm not the father," he stated and showed Grayling the results.

"See, Gray, I knew you were the father," Royce stated giddily.

Matan dropped to his knees and thanked God, then he got up and stood up to Grayling. "Congrats."

"Daddy, you should open yours too," Royale stated. She had been so quiet Matan had forgotten she was even present.

Grayling nodded and opened his envelope as well. Matan couldn't help but notice how the mood lifted. Grayling stared at the paper, his facial expression pained, which caused Matan to react.

"Bishop, are you okay?" It was if Matan hadn't even said a word because Grayling was glaring at Royce.

"Royce, who is the father?"

"Oh no. Seriously, mother?" Royale lamented, shaking her head in shame.

At least Royce looked a little embarrassed. "I used artificial insemination."

Grayling started to chuckle. It wasn't because something was funny, but more like a manic chuckle, like his wife was really on another level of psychotic. All Matan did was stand in awe and acrimony. He watched as Royale exited without another word.

"Why? What is wrong with you, Royce? You're evil. I mean, you are pure evil. Something is terribly wrong with you. What was the point of this? You nearly ruined my life. Yes, I was wrong too, but to pretend that either myself or the Bishop is the father of a baby you purposely created through artificial insemination is just low. I got to go. I can't even." He ran out of the office, leaving Grayling and Royce behind.

Grayling took a deep breath. "I don't know. I've done everything humanly possible to help you, but you just keep slapping me in the face. Do you think I'm a weak man? Do you think I'm a stupid man?" he queried, not wanting an answer. "At any time, you could have told the truth, but instead you did this. Why do you keep hurting people, Royce? What did any of us ever do to you to be on the receiving end of such malicious deceit?"

"I can't help who I am. I was desperate when I did it. Honestly,

Gray, I've tried to be better. Can't we just start over and raise this baby together? It's yours if you really think about it. We're still married."

"No."

"Gray?"

"I'm going to call Janice, your counselor, to come get you. I tried, Royce, but I'm done for real now. I'm not a licensed therapist, but you definitely have some mental issues, and you need more help than I can provide."

"I'm sorry, Gray. I really am. I don't know why I did any of it," she confessed.

*　*

Ronald woke up out of a dead sleep. His body was aching, his joints stiff. That was his osteoarthritis, but now he was dealing with bloating, nausea, and vomiting. He'd been feeling bad for a while, but he refused to go back to the doctor. They had phoned him, but he didn't have time. He was busy with rallies, recruitment, and his son. Over the course of two weeks, they had burned several Black churches, and next on their list was Holy Trinity Inter-Faith Worship Center. Khan was still defiant, and no one could find Strom.

Shaking the thought, he rolled out of bed and padded to his bathroom where he began to vomit. His head was hanging in the toilet when he felt the arrival of another person. Taking a deep breath, he slowly turned his head to see Khan standing by the door with his arms crossed, glaring at him.

"Boy, is ya going to stand there looking or help me?"

"Pop, I tried to help you. The doctor called me, and I made you an appointment for last week, which you skipped out on because the doctor isn't white. It's either that or I'm assuming you burning churches and brainwashing impressionable kids to become hate warriors was more important. You do know that you have liver cancer. I don't know what stage, but by the way you look, it may be metastatic." His son shrugged his shoulders before turning and leaving Ronald to his own devices.

Fifteen minutes later, Ronald had cleaned himself up, then he sluggishly gaited to the front room where he found his son sitting on the couch. He was all kinds of pissed at Khan. His son was an embarrassment, but at least he had come back home.

"Say what'chu gotta say, boy," Ronald snapped.

However, his son didn't open his mouth. Instead, he pulled out a paper and handed it to him.

"What's this?"

"Your one last shot to repent of your ways and let Christ have His way with you. That Christian Identity you're claiming isn't the way to God. This is a poem entitled *The Hound of Heaven*, written by Francis Thompson. Basically, the person is running from the Lord, but God won't let him go and continues to chase him. He loves him so much that He won't stop His pursuit. You need God. You need to let Him in your life because He's all you have left, Pop. I know what you did and who you are. You killed my mother and set up an innocent man because he had mom's heart and you didn't. You also killed my sister or brother she was pregnant with. Don't deny it.

"If I were the man you wanted me to become, you'd be dead now, but God is greater than you, and I've been blessed beyond belief to be surrounded by Christians, which is why you get to live. You can thank Royale and Mama Byse for your life. I love them so much.

"Royale's a good woman, a beautiful black woman who, one day, will be my wife and mother of my beautiful children. She reminded me of 1 John 4:7—"

"Shut up, Khan," he interrupted. "How dare you come in my home and disrespect me like this. I'll never thank a monkey. You got the same sickness as Strom. You pathetic waste of sperm," Ronald sneered as he attempted to get up and attack his son.

"Pop, sit. I won't fight you. We already know you'll lose. I'm just here to let you know that I'm done. One day, I'll forgive you, but not this day." Khan got up and ambled to the door and opened it.

Ronald followed, though at a turtle's pace. He was unaware that there was an audience on the other side. "I should have killed you that night too. How could you let your momma betray me like that? Huh, boy? You were a freaking race traitor since conception," Ronald snapped and then came up short when he was met by the police and the FBI. But what pissed him off was seeing Eli, Royale's grandfather.

"Oh, yeah, Pop, I meant to tell you that the authorities are here to arrest you. I bet you didn't know Wiley has been undercover this entire time. He's a better agent than Strom, that's for sure. I thought you were KBI; it's your job to make sure stuff like this doesn't happen," Khan stated smugly.

"Wiley, you rat. You monkey-sympathizing snitch," Ronald hurled before a coughing fit took him over.

"You have the right to remain silent." Ronald was pissed. He was so angry; his body was trembling.

"I win, Ronald. You should've never come for my grandbaby. You should have learned when your father failed, but you just had to try me," the General hissed with a wink before sauntering off with a smug smirk.

* *

Khan leaned back on his truck and watched with a satisfied grin as his father was handcuffed and put into the back of the squad car. Hoss had already been arrested, and some of the Knight Ryders. This would be all over the news soon. That was a good thing because hopefully, it would bring Everleigh out of hiding.

"He didn't take that too well, huh?" Nehemiah asked, leaning out of the window.

"Nah, not too well at all," Khan agreed. He was about to say more when his cell started to ring. He picked it up and saw that it was Royale and quickly answered. "I'm fine, Honey Drop."

"Thank heavens. That makes me feel better."

"What's wrong?"

"That can wait. I know you said you were fine, but how did it go? I should have been there with you."

"It's better than expected. Now, tell me what's wrong."

"Khan, I need a vacation. I know I said I wasn't running anymore, but my vessel has lost her mind."

He knew it was bad if she was back to calling her mother 'vessel' and wanted to leave. "What happened in the time that we left?"

"So, they did a DNA test earlier, and how about Matan and my dad aren't the fathers."

"Seriously? Wait, let me guess, it's Marc's."

"Possible, but she was artificially inseminated. She dragged this on and on, upsetting my dad and Matan and knew the entire time neither of them was the father. I had to get out of the office."

"Artificially inseminated? Goodness. Between your mom and Ronald, I'm not sure which one is worse. Why did she do that?"

"That's the million-dollar question. I can speculate, but I don't think she'll ever tell the truth. I wanted this to work. I wanted my mother to finally be a mom, but she's incapable of caring about anyone but herself. I'm just exhausted from all the drama."

"Yeah, babe, you're right, we need a vacation, all of us. Let's do that Canada trip."

"Okay. Oh, did you talk to Kalid?"

"Yes, he'll be a free man soon. Thanks to your grandfather, they're going to exonerate him."

"Thank the Lord for that. Khan, I'm sorry—"

"Honey Drop, don't apologize. I'm your man, I want you to always call me. Are you okay now?"

"I'll feel better when I see you with my own eyes. Is my grandfather okay? He didn't attack Ronald, did he?"

"As soon as I take care of business here, I'll be back in Virginia. The General is fine. He didn't intervene at all. I love you."

"I love you too."

Once he hung up, Nehemiah tapped his shoulder. "Dude, what did Royale's mom do now?"

"Ne, I think that woman is certifiable. She had everyone believing that either her husband or Matan fathered her child, and turns out, she's been artificially inseminated."

Nehemiah dropped his head. "She really is about that reality star life."

Khan nodded in agreement and then got into his truck and they headed back to the apartment.

* *

Khan laid beside his mother's grave and closed his eyes. He inhaled deeply and slowly exhaled. "We got him, mom. Ronald is in prison where he belongs for a long list of charges, and I know he's the one who took you from me. I'm thankful that I'm more like you than him. If I'd believed his lies, I would've never been free, never gotten saved, never found the truth, and never met Royale. These past few months have been the best and worse. Kisha was taken from us for nothing more than the color of her skin. It still baffles me. The church, where you loved to attend, as did the Byses, was burned down because of hate. I don't understand it. All of this because you loved Kalid and not Ronald, or maybe you did love Ronald, but you were in love with Kalid. I don't know, all I know is you should still be here. I love you, mom. I love everything about you, and I don't care about the past," he confessed.

For the next ten minutes, he just laid there, allowing the sun to tan his skin as he recalled the fondest memories of his mother. All his life, he felt like he was missing something, and the day he accepted Christ in his life, he felt renewed. It was that love that saved him. Had he found out his mother was taken from him because of his father before having a personal relationship with God, he'd be doing time, probably life. It amazed him how having the Spirit could be so powerful. He was in awe, but thankful. He sat up and blew a kiss to his mom and then headed back to his truck.

"How'd it go, love?" Royale queried; her long legs crossed. She was sporting some cowgirl boots, a knee length skirt, and a cute shirt. She refused to wait on him to come to Virginia and came to West Virginia. He took her all in and ambled to her and lifted her in his arms. "Well. How'd it go with Kisha?" While he visited his mother, Royale had visited Kisha.

"It was refreshing. Once the authorities find Everleigh, I'll feel much better."

He nodded in agreement. Today, he didn't want to think about all of that. He just wanted to spend the day with his lady and make her feel as special as she made him feel. "How about we go out on a date?"

"Are you sure? I thought maybe you wanted a house date."

"Nope, I want to spend the entire day with you. We deserve some us time."

"As you wish." She giggled as he began tickling her.

"Thank you, Royale, for always being around when I need you," he spoke earnestly. He gently placed her back on her feet and gazed intensely into her eyes. He lifted her face in his hands and placed a chaste kiss on her forehead, then her left cheek, followed by her right and then the tip of her nose. "Sometimes, I don't believe you're real, other times, I can hardly believe God allowed a man like me to be loved by you. It's going to get better, Royale. This kind of love we have, nothing is going to tear it down. This kind of love we have is powerful, healing, and it's ordained." She granted him a smile, and he kissed her dimples. "Love will always trump hate."

"Always," Royale replied.

* *

It had been a crazy but rewarding couple of months. Kalid was released and moved near Nina and Keith. Ronald was serving his time and getting treatment for his liver cancer, but Khan hadn't spoken to him. However, he did pray for him. Gwendolyn and Antwon were planning their nuptials, Grayling's church was growing again, and the scandal that had rocked the church was now uniting them. It was the perfect time for Khan and Royale to take their vacation. That's what they did. They were in British Columbia, hiking through Naikoon Provincial Park.

Royale surprised him and was able to get Nehemiah and Canton to come as well. They had already been in the area for two days, and Khan was having the best time. Being here brought back great memories of time spent with his mom.

Just as they were getting into the rented SUV, Royale's cell phone went off.

"Hello?"

That was all Khan heard before she started screaming, alarming them all.

"Babe, Honey Drop, what's the matter?" he queried, but she didn't reply. Concerned, he took her cell phone.

"Hello?"

"Khan, it's Patty. Um, y'all need to get back to Virginia ASAP, it's not looking good. Everleigh, she burned the church." He let out a sigh. He hated getting these phone calls. He thought it was all over now.

"Who is hurt, Patty?" he asked as he motioned for Nehemiah to assist Royale in getting inside and told Canton to drive.

"Just come to Virginia, please," Patty implored.

* *

Royale stood in her black dress singing Jennifer Hudson's "Jesus Promised Me A Home Over There". Her orotund voice shielded the weakening of her heart. Royce was gone. She had died attempting to save others from the fire that Everleigh had set at the church.

There was a blessing in this all: the doctors had saved her little brother. He was premature but alive, and her father had named him Grayland Royce Chastain. The other blessing was that Everleigh had been arrested and couldn't harm any more innocent people.

As Royale ended the song, she looked towards the congregation. There were so many mourners, her mother's castmates, the church family, and family. Then her eyes rested on her mother's closed casket and tears slid down her eyes as she recalled the letter she had pinned to her dress. Her mother was a mess inside, and Royale didn't know how disturbed her mother truly was until she read the letter Royce had left behind.

She prayed that in her mother's last moments, that she got right with Christ because she wanted to see her mother again.

Shaking the thought, she placed the microphone back on the stand and started to make her way to her seat, when Khan extended his hand and escorted her, speaking sweetly in her ear to remind her it was going to be okay.

Epilogue

Khan pulled Royale close and kissed her. She'd caught her aunt's bouquet. She wore a beautiful, deep purple bridesmaid gown that made her skin shimmer. He had been watching her the entire night. Everyone was.

Royale sang "At Last" by Etta James at the wedding, and it was lovely. It took a few months, but the church was rebuilt, and as soon as it was, Antwon and Gwendolyn set a wedding date and were finally married. The wedding was the event of the year and Khan was excited to be part of it. He had lost so much over the years that he was excited to see new life being born and new family being created.

He had yet to visit his father. He didn't hate him, but he had done all he could for him. Besides, he had a lot of men filling that role. He and Kalid were close, and they had recently gone on a father–son trip that included Canton and his father, Nehemiah and Keith, Matan and Magnus, and Bishop Grayling and Little Gray, who, although was born early, was one strong little guy and everyone loved him. He made a wonderful recovery and had his father, well, the entire family, wrapped around his little finger.

Little Gray was the glue that held the family together after Royce's death. It was a hard time, especially for Royale, but Ma Gwendolyn was there for her, as was everyone else. It was helping her father take care of her brother that prevented her from succumbing to depression. He was proud of her for that.

"You look very handsome," Royale complimented Khan and

he smiled, showcasing all his teeth and dimples.

"Thank you, sweetness. In less than a year, this is going to be us."

"You're really going to wait that long to propose to me?" she queried, holding up her bouquet.

"Babe, I signed the contract. You know the General won't budge. Did he not singlehandedly get two men out of prison and place the real murderer in prison? We still don't know where Strom is."

"That is true," she giggled, resting her head on his shoulder.

"Yeah, so we wait. Besides, you'll be busy with school and your non-profit, Far Above Rubies."

"So, you are game to come with me to Sub-Saharan Africa to save girls from becoming child brides?"

"I'm Team Royale, so I'm up for whatever."

"You're so good to me."

"As you are to me. We've been in a battle. A battle-scarred love, but our love, it's anointed."

"Amen."

*   *

Rina pouted. Did she really have to catch the bouquet? Yeah, her mother threw two, and it seemed like she purposefully meant for her and Royale to each catch one. Then, of all the people to see it, there was Canton Knight, who she decided annoyed her more than Marc. That wasn't easy to do.

"Hello, Czarina," Canton's smooth Texas drawl greeted.

She did everything in her power to ignore him, but he seemed to be just as persistent to get her to speak.

"You look very beautiful tonight. How about a dance?"

"No. I don't dance."

He frowned. She was sure he knew she was lying. She'd danced with all the men in her family, and even January's little brothers, so she clarified her statement. "I only dance with people I know."

"You know me," he replied, pulling out a chair and sitting down.

She swallowed hard. Men made her nervous, especially men like him. She didn't want to be rude because he was Khan's cousin, but she wasn't interested in him. Besides, she was still reeling from losing Royce, finding, and losing Strom, because only God and the General knew where he was, and she had unsettling feelings about having siblings out there who hated her. One so much that she tried to burn the church down with people still in it.

She couldn't lie, she noticed Canton Knight, everyone did. He was a gorgeous, successful lawyer, and he was a nice man, from what she knew of him. Royale spoke highly of him and even the General was impressed. She didn't care. Her bio-father's treatment of her taught her well. However, Canton was relentless. It was like the more she pushed away, the harder he attempted to get her attention. She wasn't having it. She took a deep breath and hopped up from her seat and sashayed off toward Grayling and the General. Canton wouldn't dare bother her now.

"What's wrong, sweetheart?" Grayling queried, looking handsome in his tux.

"Nothing, Canton just won't leave me alone. Where is Royale?"

"She and Khan are on Little Gray duty. Is Canton an issue that Antwon and I need to handle?"

"No, he's harmless, just annoying."

He nodded. "I know what Strom did to you, and the way he treated you has had a negative impact, but honey, all men aren't bad. If you're interested, it's okay to date him or anyone else. The General will do an entire background check, and ever since the situation, you girls have had security following you around. If that doesn't offer you assurance, then remember what the Bible says: God didn't give us a spirit of fear."

"I know, dad, I do, I just...I'm trying."

"Pray, and God will lead you," he advised and pulled her into an embrace.

"So, are you ready for Oxford?"

"As ready as I'll ever be."

* *

Royale smiled, which she hadn't done in a while. So much had occurred in 2015 that she didn't know if they'd make it to 2016. Here it was, a new year, and they had made it. She watched her little brother sleep on Khan's chest. It was absolutely the cutest thing she had ever witnessed. Those two were good friends. The idea of one day becoming a mother warmed her to her core. She leaned down and kissed Khan and Little Gray before putting a blanket on them.

She then got down on her knees and said a prayer. She prayed for the Byse family, her family, Khan's family, their church, and even Strom's family. As she prayed, she thought of everything her family had gone through and told God thank you. They'd been in a storm. After she prayed, she pulled out the letter her mother had written her, one she hadn't shared with anyone, the same letter she had pinned to her funeral dress, and she read it.

Dear Royale Makeda Chastain,

This is part of my therapy. I was told that writing is therapeutic so here goes. This is me telling my story to my daughter. I'm scared, but I need you to know me.

My body started decaying after it was violated, and I think that's when my mind snapped. In the early years, I didn't know what was wrong with me, but I was self-centered and overly dramatic. I worried about how I looked and craved excitement and attention, hence my need to be with men and the need to have my own reality show. I think they term that a personality disorder. I've had a mental illness I was never treated for, and it has wreaked havoc and hurt on so many innocent people. That's my fault.

I was broken long before you were born, but I thought with you, I could live life again. That somehow all the things my abuser took from me I would get back. You never get your innocence back. I thought marrying your father, an excellent man of God, would erase the shame I felt. It didn't, it only highlighted how unworthy I was. Then you came, my royal little baby girl. You and Czarina were my Royals. I wanted perfection

for you, but I fell short, not you. It was never you. Somehow, you came to represent what I lost, and what I could never be. I saw you no longer as my daughter but my competition, and I wanted to break you. I didn't. I'm glad I didn't.

I'm sorry. I know your father probably won't believe this since he thinks I'm incapable of sincere apologies. I did him so wrong, how could he ever think anything but the worse of me? However, I am sorry. I was wrong for what I did to you, Grayling, Matan, and Roslyn. I think it's true when they say hurt people, hurt people. Well, I meant to destroy you all. I hate myself for that. The truth is, Matan did and does love you. Maybe you two would have ended up married, I don't know. I will tell you this. Our first time together, I drugged him, and after that, it was easy to mess with his mind. I don't think he would have ever crossed that line without me doing what I did. I apologize for that as well. I purposely destroyed Matan as a revenge tactic to get back at his mother. Terrible, I know. So, you see, my dear love, you were all collateral damage, as was your father. It should've never happened. I can't excuse my behavior. I was evil, and I was sick in my mind and spirit.

I regret the pain I caused and how I so carelessly abused your feelings and hurt your father repeatedly. Grayling loved me until the end. He loved me until I forced him to leave me. He's a good man, and I believe your Khan is just as good as your father. Keep him, Royale. Don't do what I did. Don't allow your past to represent your entire life. Love as much and as often as you can. Seek the kingdom of God and not Man like me. I left God, turned my back on Him, but He never left me. I've been a bad mother, daughter, wife, and friend, but I pray God will forgive me, that you all will forgive me so I may see you all again in the New Jerusalem.

You, my dear daughter, are something so exquisite and rare. God gave me a wonderful blessing when He gifted me you. I was just too stupid and selfish to notice it. I see it now. I wish you and Khan a wonderful life. Don't allow anyone to break the connection you two share, never go to bed angry, always keep the lines of communication open, wake up praying together, do your quiet time together, and love each other through all seasons of life. Do your best to be what he needs, and make sure he does the same. You're a team, so work as one. Please, don't keep secrets, they only hurt more in the long run, and they always come out. There's so much I want to say, but you're a smart woman, and I know you'll do just fine. Plus, you have a wonderful support system.

I leave you with this. Do you remember that song, "I Hope You Dance" by Lee Ann Womack? Well, baby, I hope you dance, and I hope you share that song with your brother. I got a feeling I won't live to see him grow up. Please impart your wisdom on him, never let him fall for a woman like me, and teach him to love God no matter the adversity he faces. I love you both. I love you so much and I regret I didn't tell you that more. These verses, 1 John 4:7-19, I found as I repented to God and implored Him to purge my sickness. I think it's befitting to end the letter with those verses. When you read them think of me, not the woman I was, but the woman God transformed.

Love Always,
Your mother, Royce Chastain

Royale folded the note and let one tear slide down her cheek, and whispered, "I love you, momma, and I forgive you. God, instill in me this kind of love," she prayed. She blew three kisses to heaven, one for her mother, one for Kisha, and one for Khloe Masterson.

The End.

Y. Deonna's Book List & Contact Info

Goode Love Series (Inspirational Romance)

Symphony Of Goode Love

Duology (Christian Fiction-BWWM)

Battle Scarred Love 1

Battle Scarred Love-Finale

Standalone Novels (Urban Christian Fiction)

Deception Has A Name

Her Mistake, His Masterpiece

Healing A Bitter Heart

Trilogy (Urban Christian/Family Fiction)

Stolen Virtue

A Virtuous Theory

The Theory of All

Connect:

Email: authorydeonna@gmail.com

Join the new Facebook group to be in the know: Reader Group

IG: authorydeonna

https://linktr.ee/ydeonna

Facebook page: fb.me/Authorydeonna

Would you like to be a beta reader? I just created a new group just for you.

Join here.

www.ingramcontent.com/pod-product-compliance
Lightning Source LLC
Chambersburg PA
CBHW021017180626
46814CB00003B/1335